Love in Port

LESLEY LLOYD

228 Hamilton Ave.,
Palo Alto, CA 94301

ISBN 978-1-960946-05-8 (softcover)
ISBN 978-1-960946-06-5 (ebook)

This book is a work of fiction. Names, characters, places, and incidents are the product of the author's imagination or are used fictitiously. Any resemblance to actual locales, events, or persons, living or dead, is purely coincidental.

Printed in the United States of America.

Chapter 1

I went out one night with a friend of mine, Lily, and her mom as it was her mom's birthday. We went for supper at Stax Steakhouse on the beachfront in Durban.

After a delicious meal, we decided to go and watch a cabaret at the Malibu Hotel at a place called Port O' Call. When we got there, we bumped into a few of Lily's friends. I was not too chuffed as I knew I would not get on with them. Then Lily turned to me and asked me to go and get her a cigarette.

I scanned the bar and saw only one guy, so I walked over to the bar and looked to see if he was a smoker. He looked hot with black hair and piercing eyes. I moved over to his side of the bar and asked him if I could have a cigarette. He looked at me and spoke a different language. I pointed to the pack of cigarettes, and he clicked, and I took one out of the packet.

He then lit it for me, and I said, "I am coming back now." I walked back to Lily and gave her the cigarette. I then came back to the bar, and we started talking in broken English. I learnt that his name was Edmondo, and he was working for the Mediterranean Shipping Company, and their ship had engine trouble. Anyway, after talking for a while, I invited him to join our table. He said yes and walked back with me.

Lily was surprised to see me with a guy, and I introduced him to the other people at our table. Then after the cabaret, which was good, they put dancing music on. I was happy, and Ed and I got up and started dancing. We danced for quite a while. Eventually, Lily and her friends said goodbye, and Lily came to the table. Ed asked if we would like to go for coffee somewhere. I said yes straight away, and Lily and her mom followed.

We ended up at a little coffee shop around the corner from the hotel and sat chatting for some time. I thought Ed was a great guy. I could see Lily wasn't too chuffed with me and couldn't care less.

Eventually, we left, and Ed walked with us to Lily's car. He took my phone number and said he would catch a taxi back to the ship. We said goodbye, and Lily drove off. We dropped her mom at home, and then Lily took me home as she was sleeping over at my place. Lily and I had been working together selling timeshare, but I had just got a new job working for stockbrokers in the middle of town. I had only been working there for about two weeks and was very happy there.

We got to my house, and Lily asked me about Ed, and I told her he was a second lieutenant on a ship. He was from Naples and spoke Italian. She thought I was crazy to like him as he could not speak such great English. I said that did not worry me. We went to sleep, and I was up early to sort out my two-year-old son. I used to get a lift with my dad to work as he worked in town. That morning in the car, he asked why I was in such a good mood, and I told him Lily, her Mom, and I had a great time out for her mom's birthday. I mentioned meeting Edmondo, and he said I must be careful of men like that as they sometimes have woman in every port.

I was not fazed by what my dad said. I got to work and went out to the shops at lunchtime. I got back to the office, and then the phone rang. I picked it up, and this person asked to speak to Rae in a foreign accent. I knew it was Ed straight away. I asked if his name was Edmondo, and he said yes, and he asked when we could meet.

I said, "Why don't you come into town and meet me at the Royal Hotel?" Which was right next to the building I worked in. He said all right, and we met there after work. He looked so sexy in a denim shirt and had a great aftershave on. We went and had a drink, then I said I had to catch the bus home. He said he would come with me. I told him about my son Ross, and he didn't seem to mind. He was keen to meet my folks. We walked from the Royal Hotel to the bus stop, and on the way, we passed Peters Flowers on the side of the road. Ed went up and bought me a bunch of red roses. I was so surprised, and here I was, getting on the bus with a man and roses. Everyone in the bus started making comments about me and Ed with the roses. Eventually, after being on the bus for about half an hour, I had enough, so we both got off at the next stop, as there was a shortcut I knew we could walk to get to my house.

We got home to my folks where I lived with my son, Ross. I introduced Ed to my mom who was at home with my son. Then I made Ross supper, and we sat outside, and Ed fed it to him. He was so taken aback with my son as he had blond hair, and Italians are all black-haired. Anyway, after that, Ed had supper with my folks, and he and I seemed to get on with my mom and dad really well. We then drove Ed back to the ship.

Ed phoned me every day after that, and during the weekends, we got together. He invited me to go out and watch a cabaret with him and some of his mates from the ship. We ended up at the Beach Hotel at Ruby Tuesdays. I found myself falling in love with Ed. He was such a loving guy and so patient with my son. It was coming up for Valentine's Day, and Ed could not get off on Valentine's Day, which was on a Saturday, so we decided to celebrate on Friday. Ed said I must hire a car so that I could take him to see Valley of 1000 Hills up near Bothas Hill.

Just before Valentine's Day, Ed invited me to come for supper on the ship. I went after work, and the captain invited us to sit with him at the captain's table. It was a great evening, and he said I must bring my son so he could show him the ship. I said I would do that as soon as I could.

On the Friday, I hired a Sentra car and met Ed. He wanted to go and look at the shops at the workshop so we stopped there, and Ed bought me a soft red-and-white toy. We then went and had photos taken of the two of us. Then we drove up to Valley of a 1000 Hills. It was beautiful up there, and Ed and I had a drink and stood looking out at the outstanding view. Ed said it was awesome.

After that, we drove down Fields Hill and to my place in La Lucia. When we got to my place, the folks were not home, so Ed and I had a shower and got dressed. I had bought Ed some white jeans that fitted him perfectly. We were so excited about that night and waited for my folks to come home. They chatted to us. I fed Ross, and then we said goodbye and left.

We drove to Gordon's Prawn to have supper. I knew the owner of the restaurant, and he gave us a good table near the dance floor. We had our supper and danced and chatted. After that, I said, "Let's drive to the beachfront and go to Raffles Night Club." Ed was so keen, so off we went. When we got to Raffles, there were a few people dancing, and there was a glassed-off part of the restaurant that looked onto the dance floor. We had a drink, and then we got up and danced.

Ed was wearing white pants, and with the lights, they glowed in the dark of the club. At one stage, we were shuffling by ourselves on the dance floor.

It felt so special, and we both didn't want to go home. Then Ed suggested we go and book into the Oyster Box Hotel in Umhlanga Rocks. We got there, and Ed surprised me by booking a garden suite. It was magnificent.

We were both so hot and sweaty from dancing, so we had a shower each. Afterward, I got out, and Ed was in his towel and sitting on the bed. I went over to him, and he kissed me and then said, "Tomorrow, we should fetch Ross and take him to the ship with us so he can see it."

I said, "Yes, that is a great idea."

He then pulled me over to him and kissed me again. The next thing I knew, we were in bed together, and Ed was running his hands up and down my sides.

Eventually, he laid me on my back, looked into my eyes, and said, "Amore." Then he lowered himself, guiding himself into me. I let out a little moan as he entered me. We rocked, and Ed did small movements, slowly arousing me, all the while keeping his eyes on me. I thought he was so strong, I skimmed my hands over his chest, and then he crushed my lips with his as he came and shuddered. And at the same, I time erupted and still couldn't believe we had made love. After that, we fell asleep in each other's arms.

When we woke up with the wakeup call that morning, we hugged each other. It felt strange to wake up with Ed next to me. We had some tea, then both of us had a shower and thought we had better get back to my place and fetch Ross and then go to the ship. Ed only had to be back at the ship by 11:00 a.m. that morning. We hugged each other before leaving our love nest.

We drove home, and when we got through the door, all was quiet at first. Then I heard that Ross was awake, so I went up the stairs. Ed took a seat in the lounge. He said he was going to tell my mom what had happened, and I said that was a good idea.

I got Ross and my mom called me and I said when she was ready Ed and I would like to speak to her downstairs. I got back downstairs with Ross, and Ed told him we were taking him to see the big ship he works on. Ross was so excited. I made us some coffee and then my mom came into the room. Ed just said that him and I were in love, and we had spent the night together at the Oyster Box Hotel as it was Valentine's Day today, and he could not get off. He said that we both wanted to take Ross to see the ship. My mom was not too pleased about this at first. She spoke to Ed and said it was all okay with him and I, but she didn't feel going to the ship was a place for a child. I said that is tough; we have already spoken to Ross, and he is excited about going. My mom eventually consented to letting us go, and I went upstairs to change myself and Ross and pack a bag to go out with. My mom said she would fetch Ross and I at the workshop at 4:00 p.m.

I could not wait to get out the house as was so tired of explaining everything to the folks. I appreciated what they did for Ross and me but just felt sometimes they smothered us.

Ed was so understanding, and as I drove us all into town, I was a bit disappointed that we couldn't have gone back to the Oyster Box Hotel for breakfast with Ross as well.

Ed also said that that would have been great. I realized I had fallen head over heels in love with Ed.

We got to the car hire place in Aliwal Street and handed in the car. I put Ross in his stroller; and Ed, Ross, and I walked down to the ship, which was near the esplanade.

We got to the ship, and the captain came up to us and asked to pick Ross up and show him the ship. We said yes, and Ross had a good time with the captain.

Ed and I went into the cabin and chatted about our relationship and looked at the photos we had taken the night before. We could hardly keep our hands off each other. We got up and went to find the captain who could not get over Ross's blond hair. We had some coffee with him, then Ed had to get to work. Ross and I eventually left, and Ed walked us down the gang plank. He said he would phone me later that night at home.

I said thanks for everything as we really had a lovely time together. Ross and I walked to the workshop, and when we got there, there was some fashion show on which we watched. Ross fell asleep in the stroller, and before I knew it, it was 4:00 p.m., and I had to meet my mom.

We met my mom, and she apologized for creating such a scene in taking Ross to the ship. She asked if we had a good time. I said, "We sure had and Ross had a great time, and he enjoyed the big ship."

We drove home, and when we got home, Ross woke up. My mom said she would give him some tea and a biscuit. I said, "Great, then I am going to have a nap." My mom woke me up at 6:30 p.m., and I came downstairs and helped my mom with supper.

My dad had come home from golf and was talking to Ross. We ate supper and then were sitting in the lounge when Ed phoned. I spoke to him, and he asked if I could get a lift into town to the ship tomorrow afternoon as he had the night off. I said I would ask my folks and he must phone me in the morning so I could tell him.

He agreed to do that, and then he said, "Amore." And I just melted into the phone and said, "I love you."

Chapter 2

I met Ed the next day at the Royal Hotel after work. He asked me if I could get off from work and come with him on the ship as far as Cape Town. I said I would have to ask my boss the next day. He said it would be great if I could do that as then we could be together longer. I said I would try my best and see what I could do.

The next day at work, I spoke to my boss about going to Cape Town. He told me I could go. I was so excited I could hardly wait to tell Ed after work. As soon as 4:30 p.m. came, I ran out the door and ran into Ed's arms as he was waiting for me at the Royal Hotel. I just said I can come to Cape Town. He was so happy he just said, "That is great, Rae!"

We went to a bar and had a drink, and he said he would have to get my papers sorted out with the ship as soon as possible as the ship was leaving for Cape Town the next week. I said, "Okay, that is great. I will give you my passport and then see if they will sort out my papers."

We chatted a little more then left and walked to catch the last bus home. When we got home, I left Ed talking to Ross and my mom and upstairs to get my passport to give to Ed. We had a great evening.

The next day, I could not wait to see Ed. He took me out to dinner in Umhlanga Rocks. As we were sitting there, having a glass of wine, he told me that unfortunately, the papers would take two weeks to process. I was so disappointed. Ed got up and hugged me and said we will just have to make the most of our time together.

We enjoyed our dinner together then caught a taxi back to my home. Once there, my dad and I took Ed back to the ship.

The next day, Ed said I must hire the car again two days before he leaves for Cape Town. He said he was going to take us out to Gordon's Prawn, and then we would spend the night at the Oyster Box again. I was thrilled so I booked the car for the next day and booked the night at the Oyster Box.

The day arrived when I was to hire the car so I left work and met Ed at the Royal Hotel. We walked to get the car in Aliwal Street. We drove off in the car to the Umhlanga Rocks beach. We took a long walk along the promenade past the light house and then went back to the car. We then drove to my house and saw Ross and fed him his dinner, and then Ed read him a story while I had a shower and told Ross we would see him tomorrow. After that, we chatted to the folks for a while then left to go to Gordon's Prawn.

We had a lovely evening; we shared a platter of prawns and langoustines and danced to the lovely music. It was about 10:30 p.m. once we had finished our coffees so we left and went to the Oyster Box Hotel. We checked in and had a lovely room on the first floor overlooking the beach. We made passionate love, and afterward, I lay in Ed's arms saying how much I was going to miss him. He said it wouldn't be too long, and he would be back with me. I said, "You will have to phone me as often as you can."

He said he would then we fell asleep.

The next day, he had a day off, and I had taken the day off to say goodbye to him. We showered and went down to breakfast where they had a delicious spread of fruits and yoghurt. We ate and then took a walk on the promenade again and drove home and took Ross down to the beach with us. We left the beach at lunchtime as had to go home, have lunch, then leave to see Ed off at the ship.

By the time we left my home to take Ed to the ship, Ross was tired, so we left him with my mom. Ed said goodbye to Ross, and we left home for the ship.

We got to take the car back, and all was good. Then we walked to the ship, and I hugged and kissed Ed goodbye. He said he would phone me from Cape Town. Then I turned and left him standing there, watching me walk away to get the bus home.

Chapter 3

The day after Ed left, I woke up went to see if Ross was awake in his bedroom, and as I got there, I saw his smiling face, which warmed my heart. He said, "Mom, what we gonna do today?"

I almost burst out crying as I was still feeling minus emotional after Ed's leaving and myself not being able to go with on the ship to Cape Town.

So Ross and I walked downstairs together and went and played some soccer outside on the grass.

A little while later, we both came inside, and my mom said, "Let's sit down and have some breakfast." So we did that and I had no interest in food but ate some muesli anyway.

After that, Ross and I got ready as we had decided to go to the beach near the rock pools.

I got some cold drinks for us for us in our own bottles and something to munch, grabbed the towels, put them in our beach bag, and started walking as the beach was across the road.

As we got out the gate, we saw two cyclists going past and then crossed the road.

It was a great sunny day with not a cloud in the sky. We chose our spot on the beach near this dugout and put on some suntan lotion. As I glanced out at the sea and saw the boats on the horizon, I immediately thought of Ed. Gee! I sure missed him so much already. They were in Cape Town, and I was hoping that he would phone me that night.

Ross and I built a sandcastle and had fun running around the beach, throwing a ball to each other and kicking a soccer ball.

By the time we got home, I was exhausted and so was Ross. I made us a sandwich, and after that, Ross and I fell asleep on my bed in my bedroom.

When we woke up, it was like 4:00 p.m., so I made us both some tea. My mom was in the kitchen too, so she also had tea with us.

After that, Ross went to kick his soccer ball outside, and I joined him we were just trying to pass time. At about 5:00 p.m., I brought him inside and took him to have a bath. When he was all clean, I brought him back downstairs and let him watch some TV while I made his supper.

I fed him at about 6:00 p.m., and he ate all his food, which I was glad about. At about 6:30 p.m., the phone rang, and it was Ed. I was so chuffed I had picked it up. We chatted about everything and how much we both missed each other. He had bought me an Italian dictionary, and I was going to try and write to him in Italian.

The weeks went by the daily work a world, and commuting on the bus only brought back more memories of Edmondo.

It was going toward October, and I got a letter from Ed to say his ship would be in Durban on November 8, 1988.

I was so delighted to hear this news that I got off the bus and had such a lot of happiness and joy in my step as I walked home from work, and when I got back, I told Ross and swung him into the air. He giggled with glee!

November 8 was a Tuesday, and I had taken the afternoon off. My mom kindly brought Ross in to fetch me from work, and we drove to the container terminal. Ross was ecstatic, and I was beaming with love and apprehension.

We got out the car and walked to the steps of the MSC ship and stood there like Ed had asked us to do at the exact time 3:30 p.m. All of a sudden, I looked up the stairs and saw him at the top in his white uniform. He dashed down those steps so fast and picked Ross into the air and hugged all three of us. My, what a heart-warming experience. I stood their entranced. It was like the Julia Roberts movie almost, *An Officer and a Gentleman.*

He then gathered his thoughts, put Ross down, took my face in both his hands, and kissed me so that a tingling sensation coursed throughout my body, and I just kissed him back hungrily.

We then walked hand in hand to the car, and he hugged my mom. After we got inside, he asked if I could book a table at Gordon's Prawn as he remembered it from our valentine evening.

I got home and could not stop looking at Ed. He went to feed Ross and told me to go and shower quickly. I listened and got into a turquoise dress and bronze sandals. I came downstairs, and Mom said he was in the office talking to Dad. I said can I join them, and she said yes. Ross was eating at the highchair. I moved into the office, but before I got there, I heard him asking my dad a lot of questions and realized they were about me.

I then knocked, and they both said, "Come in!"

I walked in and sat next to Ed on the couch. He had a huge smile on his face, and I wondered what else I had missed. Then I told him we had fifteen minutes to get to the Gordon's Prawn. He then stood up and pulled me toward him in a hug. My dad said we must have a lovely time, and we walked out. Ed lifted Ross out of the highchair, and we both settled him on the couch, hugged, and kissed him good night.

We arrived at Gordon's Prawn and got a lovely, secluded cozy table in the corner. We sat down, and Gordon came over in his friendly way and welcomed us to his restaurant. Then we ordered some wine and sat, holding hands, eyes still locked on each other's face. We were both amazed that we were back together after six months apart.

They started playing a Whitney Houston song, which I loved, so we just looked at each other and got up without a word and sauntered over to the dance floor. To feel his embrace was so warm, it thrilled me throughout my being. It was as if we glided in time to the music and were the only couple on the floor although we were not.

After that we went to sit down as Ed had ordered oysters to share as a starter. I got to the table and sat down. As I did, Ed sat down and purposefully got a fork and doctored an oyster for me. I just happened to glance down before opening my mouth when I saw something sparkle just once. I put my hand toward the fork and looked deep into Edmondo's eyes. He said, "Will you marry me?"

I was so taken aback I looked at him stunned for a minute. Then I just smiled and nodded my head as was too emotional. He put the fork down, took the ring out, and wiped it on his serviette, and then took my hand and slipped the ring on my hand. We picked up our wine glasses said, "Salud!"

We kissed each other with not a care who was looking or not. As we came round and released each other, I felt I had lost my desire to eat. All I wanted to do was nibble and kiss Ed.

We eventually pulled ourselves together and took turns feeding each other the oysters. The next thing we heard was Gordon's voice talking on the microphone from the DJ area, and he announced that we had gotten engaged, and he played "For Your Eyes Only." We got up and did the shuffle around the floor, and I felt like I was floating on a cloud, and life could not get better. We had an Irish coffee, and Gordon came around and hugged and shook Ed's hand, congratulating us. He said the Irish coffee was on the house.

We left Gordon's, and Ed said we are going to go back to the Oyster Box and stayed the night, and this time, we will stay for breakfast. He did not have to be back at the ship till the next day midday. When we got to the Oyster Box Hotel, we booked a lovely room inside the hotel building this time. When we got to our room, we were so tired and I still felt like I was floating on a cloud. I phoned my mom and told her where we were staying, and she was okay with it.

Ed and I got into bed naked and made love. I fell asleep in his arms so satisfied. I thought that soon, I will be able to sleep next to him every night. We awoke the next morning to a knock on the door as we had asked for room service of coffee. I got up and put on the white gown that the hotel provides and went to open the door. Ed sat up in bed, and I came back and gave him his coffee. He took it and put it on the side table next to the bed, and then he looked at me and said, "Come here." I got back into bed, and the next thing, I was in his arms and he was kissing me. We then pulled ourselves together, and I put my hand out so Ed could look at my ring, and I turned to him and said, "Are you happy?"

And he looked at me with so much love in his eyes and said, "Yes, very, and you?"

I said, "I had never been happier."

We then made love again, and after that, we got up and had a shower together. We got dressed as this time, we had come prepared. After that, we walked downstairs and went to have breakfast on the veranda. I had phoned my work to say I would not be coming in, and they were all right with that. I sat down, and Ed took my hand with the ring on it and smiled at me. I thought I could not be happier or more fulfilled.

After we ate our breakfast, Ed said he was going to phone his mom in Naples. So we went and phoned her, and I said hello in the little bit of Italian I knew. She sounded happy for Ed and me, and she said she would like to meet me sometime. I said that would be lovely, and then I said goodbye. Ed spoke a bit more to her and was smiling when he put the phone down. He said, "We will have to see about you coming over to meet her in Naples sometime."

I said, "Yes, that would be great!"

After breakfast, we left. We caught a taxi back to my house. Ed said he was going to spend the whole day with me. My mom was glad to see us and kissed and hugged us, congratulating our engagement. She looked at my ring and liked it very much. She had not sent Ross to school so he came running in from outside and hugged Ed and me. I said, "How about we pack a picnic lunch and go down to the beach with Ross, and we can build sandcastles in the sand?"

Ed liked that idea, and so did Ross. My mom said she would take us in the car and drop us off and pick us up later. Ed told her he only had to be at the ship the next day midday. My mom said that was great. We took Ross and his bucket and spade and the picnic basket down to the beach; it was a lovely, sunny day. Ed had baggies on that I had bought him just the other day, and they fitted him perfectly. I had my costume on, and Ross had a little speedo on.

When we got to the beach, we found a lovely spot on the soft sand. I laid our towels out, and Ed and Ross started to kick the ball they had bought with them. I got up and joined them, and we had such fun just kicking the ball to each other. Then we all ran down to the water, and Ed and I held Ross's hand as we jumped over the little waves. After that, we walked back to our towels, and I got an Energade drink out for each of us and a roll I had made for us each. We ate and drank and chatted, and I thought life couldn't get better.

The sun was warm on our bodies but not scorching, but Ed thought we should put on sunscreen, so he put some on Ross's shoulders and then rubbed some on mine. I then rubbed some on his and put some on Ross's nose and cheeks. We then went closer to the water and made some sandcastles. By the time we got back to our towels and looked at the time, it was time to meet my mom. We got up, packed up our things in the bags we had bought, and then Ed picked up one back threw it over his arm and picked up Ross with the other arm, and I picked up the other bag and held Ed's hand, and we walked up to the place where we had to meet my mom. It had been a lovely day, and one I will always remember.

By the time we got back to my house, Ross was fast asleep in my arms. Ed carefully picked him up and carried him upstairs to his bed. He came downstairs, and we made some coffee and had it sitting outside with my mom. We chatted about the wedding, which we both said we would like to have in six months' time.

Ed asked if he could fly me to Naples to meet his mom, and my mom agreed with him. We decided I should go the end of the month as it was March now. I said I would speak to my boss at work the next day. I was so excited. I could not believe that soon, I would be Mrs. Lamparella.

After our coffee, Ed and I felt tired, so we went to lie down on my bed as my room was outside off the kitchen. We asked my mom to wake us in an hour as that was when I had to wake Ross otherwise he would not sleep that night.

As I turned to Ed, he took me in his arms and kissed me like never before. I gazed into his eyes and asked him if he was happy, and he said, "What a question." That he had never been happier. We then laid down on the bed and, within minutes, were asleep.

Chapter 4

When Ed and I woke up an hour later, we heard Ross and my mom in the kitchen talking. I stretched, and Ed hugged me and we got up. I could not stop looking at my ring on my finger everytime I could. Ed just stood there, smiling. He said, "I am so happy with you and can't wait for you to meet my mom and come to Naples to see my other family."

I said, "Yes, I can't wait either."

We walked into the kitchen together, and just a moment later, my dad walked in the front door from the office. We said hello, and he hugged me and shook Ed's hand. Ross was in his high chair as he was about to eat as my mom had made his supper. My dad said, "When you finished with Ross, let's have a drink and go and sit outside. It is such a lovely evening."

We finished feeding Ross, and Ed had a beer, and I had a glass of wine, and my dad poured my mom, a gin and tonic. We all went outside and sat down. My dad toasted Ed and me on our engagement, and we all chatted about the wedding and where it should be and that it was just going to be family and a few friends. Ed and I agreed with him on a small wedding and thought it would be more intimate we felt a hundred guests was more than enough. Ed said he was going to fly his mom and sister over.

My dad said that was great and that they could stay at a hotel in Umhlanga Rocks that was not too expensive. Everything was working out well. My mom said Ed must eat with us as he did not have to be back at the ship until the next day. My dad said it was okay for Ed to sleep over as we were engaged now. I just went to my dad and hugged him and thanked him. My heart felt so full of love I thought it would burst. Ross was playing with Ed with a ball on the grass they were kicking to each other with, and I chatted with my dad telling him about our day at the beach. My mom went inside to sort out the curry and rice she just had to warm it as it was made already. I then went inside to set the table for us all.

My mom said, "You better let Ross sit with us when we eat as he is so wide awake now." I agreed with her.

By the time we sat down to eat, I was hungry as Ed and I had such a lovely day together—the first time we had spent the whole night and day with each other. We ate, and Ed enjoyed the curry and rice as I thought he might find it hot for his mouth. But I was wrong, and he liked it. Then I told Ross he had to say good night to everyone, and I took him upstairs to bed. Ed came with me, and I read him a story on pirates from one of his books, and then we hugged and kissed him and put the light off. He looked content lying there.

Ed and I went downstairs and sat in the lounge with my mom and dad, chatting. Ed was telling us about his sister and the rest of his family. He had lost his dad two years ago as he had a heart attack at the age of sixty-five. We listened to Ed talking, and I loved the sound of his voice in his broken English. We looked at the time, and it was ten o'clock already. My mom and dad said they were going to bed. I said Ed and I were going to listen to some music, then we would be going to bed. They said all right and went upstairs.

I turned to Ed, and we hugged, then I got up and put a CD on. This Italian music by Andrea Bocelli filled the room. I loved opera music, and Bocelli was my favorite. Ed took me in his arms and kissed me. I was swept away in the kiss, and the music it felt surreal. I had never been happier and thought life could not get any better.

Later, we got up and went to bed together as I slept in the outside room off the kitchen. We were so tired after our long day together that we fell asleep in each other's arms.

The next day, we got up, and I left Ed having a shower while I went to find Ross and made Ed and I some coffee. I came downstairs with Ross, changed for school, and he and I went to find Ed. He was dressed when we saw him, and he came inside to have his coffee. He was going to come with us to take Ross to school then get off with me in town and come and see my office then go and catch the taxi to the ship.

By the time we were all ready to leave with my dad in the car, it was 7:15 a.m., and we kissed my mom goodbye and got into the car. Ross was so happy that he could show Ed where he went to school. We stopped at the school, and Ross asked if Ed would come inside to see it. We asked my dad, and he said it was all right with him. Ed and I got out the car with Ross and went inside the school. The school was called Valling, and the teacher came toward us and said "Good morning." We answered "Good morning too," and I introduced Ed to her. Then Ross took Ed's hand and showed him where he sat; he also showed him where they played soccer. After that, we had to leave; otherwise, I would be late for work. We both kissed Ross and hugged him, then we went to get back in the car. I felt so happy and fulfilled as I sat there being driven to work.

My dad dropped me off near the Royal Hotel, and Ed and I got out and walked into the building where my work was. We got into the lift and caught it to the floor I worked on. We both got out and walked into my office. I said good morning to everyone and then saw my boss, so I introduced Ed to him. His name was David Bennett, then Ed and I walked through to my office. I was lucky to have my own office. We both sat down, and Ed said what a stunning view I had from my window of the yachts, which was true. I then said that I had to start working, and Ed said he was going to go, and that now I was a part of him as I had a ring on. I agreed with him. I hugged him, and he kissed me and then left.

I got into my work, and Zuleika came through from the front office a little while later and said that Ed looked like such a good man. She admired my ring, and I told her we were very happy together. She asked when we were going to get married, and I said, "The end of the year, hopefully in December."

I mentioned to her that he wanted me to go to Naples hopefully soon, so she suggested that maybe I should go and talk to my boss, David, that day. I said I would, and then we got back to work.

Just before I went to lunch, David came into my office to speak about some portfolios I was doing. After we finished talking business, I told him Ed and I were planning to get married in December. He said congratulations and was happy for me. I mentioned that he wanted me to go to Naples to meet his mother and that could I go like next month for two weeks. He said he did not see a problem as we would be finished the big portfolio I was working on with him. He said he would get me leave forms to fill out. I must go ahead and make arrangements.

I caught the bus home that night all happy that things had worked out so well at work. When Ed phoned me that night and I told him what my boss had said, he was delighted and said we must go and see a travel agent so that we can sort it all out. I asked if he was going to come with me, and he said that the ship was going back to Naples in another week, and he would meet me there.

On the Saturday, Ed was off from the ship, and he phoned on the Friday night, and I said I would meet him the next morning at the Royal Hotel. I took Ross in his stroller, and we caught the bus to town from my place as the bus stops right in front of our house. We got to town, and I put Ross in his stroller, and we walked to the Royal Hotel Ed was waiting outside and looked happy to see us. We then walked together to the travel agent who were in the building a block away. We got there, and I introduced him to Fawn. She asked when we wanted to go, and I told her it was just me. She said I would have to fly to Rome and could get a train or bus to Naples. Ed said no, that he would meet me and drive me to Naples. So we booked my flight for May 25, 1986. To leave Durban and arrive back two weeks later on June 8, 1986. She told us how much it would be, and Ed asked if we could pay half now as he had the money on him. He paid, and she said that when we paid the balance, she would give me the ticket. I had to get a visa, which she said she would organize. I gave her my passport, and she said we would be in touch.

Ed, Ross, and I left and walked to the Three Monkeys Coffee Shop and had something to eat and drink. Ed said he would phone his mother from the ship and tell her. He said he was leaving on the following Wednesday, May 8, 1986, on the ship and would be back in Naples in two weeks. I said that was good, then it wouldn't be long and I would be flying out to visit them all. He looked really happy as he held my hand, and Ross had fallen asleep in his stroller.

We caught the bus back to my house, and Ed held Ross on the bus as he was fast asleep in his arms. I felt so close to Ed as we sat on the bus and felt really happy and content with the two people I loved most in the world.

We got home, and Ross had woken up, so when we got off at the bus stop, we opened the stroller and put Ross in it. I pushed it home as Ed walked next to me. As we came in the door at home, my mom walked out the kitchen and said how about a cup of a tea. I said, "Yes, please," so did Ed and Ross. We sat on the veranda having our tea and biscuits. We told my mom what had happened at the travel agents and said I would be leaving on May 25, 1986. She said, "Good, at least you will be here for my birthday on May 18, 1986."

I said, "Yes, I will be here." Ed said he would not be as he was leaving on Wednesday, May 8, 1986, with the ship to go back to Naples; and they would be in Naples in two weeks' time. My mom said that that was a pity, but she was glad I was going over to meet his mom and Ed agreed with her.

After that, Ed asked my mom if it would be okay if he took me out to dinner, and we left Ross with her and my dad. She said that of course, it would be okay. She would drop us off wherever we wanted to go. I was happy and went upstairs to shower. Ed went and gave Ross a bath while I was showering. My mom went off and made some supper for Ross. I got out the shower and put on some black pants and a floral shirt and my black sandals. I came downstairs, and Ross was in his pajamas, and Ed was helping him eat in the kitchen. Ross was sitting in his high chair. I was so happy I kissed Ed on the cheek and thanked him for bathing Ross. We asked my mom to take us to Granada Center, and we would go and have some supper at Angelos, an Italian restaurant.

My mom took us in her car and dropped us in outside Granada Center, and Ed and I got out of the car and held hands as we walked toward the restaurant. We got a lovely corner table right away, and Ed ordered some red wine for us. I was glad to be with Ed, and he held my hand and gazed at my ring. I was so in love and just looked into Ed's eyes. We looked at the menu, and I decided to have some pasta with seafood in it. Ed said he would have the same so we ordered and then sat chatting about me going to Naples in a less than a month's time. Ed asked me where I would like to live when we are married, and I said "Durban" as Ross was happy in his school, and if we had to go live overseas, there would be a language problem. He agreed with me, and we chatted about where we could find a place to stay. Ed said he could speak to his boss and ask for a land job so that he would not have to travel on the ship all the time. I said that would be great, only if he wanted to do that. He said, for me, he would do anything.

I said, then he should speak to his boss as I know MSC has a big office in the middle of town. I said we could think of getting our own car, and Ed agreed. Our food arrived, and we ate, and Ed ordered another glass of wine for us each. It was great being with Ed and knowing that I would be going over to meet his family soon. After we had eaten, Ed and I took a stroll around the center, and then it was time to meet my mom, so we waited for her, and it wasn't long when she arrived. We both got in the car, and my mom drove us home. Ed was sleeping over again as he was due back at the ship in the morning 11:00 a.m. When we got home, I went upstairs and kissed Ross who was fast asleep. I then came downstairs and made Ed and I some decaffeinated coffee. We sat outside drinking it as it was a lovely evening. My mom had gone to bed, so it was just us two. Ed said he was so happy that we were getting married, and his mom would just have to accept the fact that I was not a Catholic. I agreed with him.

Chapter 5

On the Sunday, my folks drove Ed back to the ship with Ross and me in the car as well. We dropped him off, and he said he would phone me as he was leaving on the Wednesday to go back to Naples. I kissed him goodbye, and he walked across to the ship. My folks then took Ross and I to lunch at Stax Steakhouse on the beachfront. We first walked along the beachfront as it was a little early, and then at 12:00 p.m., we walked into the restaurant. It was one of my best places to eat. We sat down and all decided to have the buffet, which was great salads to die for and meat as well. Ross and I got up and went to cut some garlic bread; it was hot as had just come out the oven. It was delicious, and we ate two slices each as it was French bread, so the slices were small.

After lunch, my dad drove us home, and Ross did some Lego while I read my book. Ed phoned to say he would meet me for lunch the next day, being Monday, as we would have to go and pay for the rest of my ticket with Fawn at the travel agents. I said great I would meet him at 1:00 p.m. in front of my building where I worked he said okay. That night, I chatted with Ross and my mom and Dad about my trip to Italy; they were very happy for me.

On the Monday, I went to work with my dad, and Ross went to school and all was well in my world. At work, my boss, David, came to me and said that my two weeks of leave had been approved, and I was very happy. He chatted to me for a while, and we did some work together on a big portfolio for the Standard Bank.

At 1:00 p.m., I was outside, and Ed was already waiting for me. He hugged me and kissed me on the cheek. Then he took my hand, and we walked to the travel agent. Fawn was happy to see us, and she said all was in order she was just waiting to get my passport back with my visa for Italy in it, but that it should arrive sometime this week and would phone me as soon as it did. Ed paid the balance of the money, and we said goodbye. I told him my leave at work had been approved and he was so happy. We went to the Royal Hotel Coffee Shop and had a toasted sandwich and a cup of coffee. Ed said could he come home with me and spend the night with my folks and Ross as he would not see us again before he left.

I, of course, said yes. He said he was going to do some shopping and would meet me at the Royal Hotel at 4:30 p.m. so that we could go and catch the bus together. I said, "Great, I will be waiting." He then walked me back to my office and sat down in the chair opposite me and said, "Gee! I sure am going to miss you and Ross." I said it will only be two weeks and I will be flying over. He said he knows, but it is still going to be lonely at sea without me. Then he left to go shopping. He said he was going to walk to the workshop as he wanted to buy a souvenir for his mom and sister. I walked him to the lift, hugged him, and went back to my office.

I finished work just after four o'clock and then caught the lift to the ground floor. I was at the Royal Hotel waiting for Ed at exactly 4:30 p.m. as discussed. I had just got their when I looked up and saw Ed walking along with a packet in each hand. He smiled at me, and my heart leapt in my chest. He was so good-looking, and in six months, he would be my husband. I could hardly believe it. He kissed me on the lips, and I hugged his neck. He had his hands full with packages. We then started walking to the bus. I offered to take a package, but he would not let me.

He said, "No peeking."

I said, "What have you done? Don't tell me you have bought us presents?"

He said, "Wait and see."

We walked past the flower sellers, and he bought me yellow roses, my favorites. I was so surprised and overjoyed that I stood there hugging him on the pavement. We got to the bus, and it was just arriving so stood in the line to get a ticket. We got on the bus and found a seat, so Ed put the packages down in front of him. I felt so proud to be with this good-looking man; a few looks came our way as people got on, and they looked at me holding my gorgeous flowers. I felt really spoilt.

We got off the bus, and Ed took his two packets off the bus, and I took my lovely roses, and we walked home. When we got home, my mom came to the door with Ross, and we kissed and hugged each other. I had phoned my mom to tell her Ed would be coming for supper, and she was happy. I was so glad my folks liked Ed; it sure made my life a lot easier. Ed picked up Ross and said he must go and sit outside as he had something to give him. Ross ran outside, and I put the kettle on for a cup of tea. We all sat outside, and Ed took a box out of the packet and gave it to Ross; it was a Lego set. Ross's eyes got big as he took the box; it was a whole Lego car that had to be built, and he was delighted. He hugged Ed, and I saw Ed's eyes get full as he hugged him back. Then he sat down in the lounge and started building it. I quickly made the tea as Ed helped Ross build his car in the lounge. My mom was very touched by Ed giving Ross the Lego car as was I. I came through to the lounge, and Ed said, "I have something to give you and your mom and dad."

I said, "You are very naughty." He said that we had been so good to him while he was in Durban that this was just a small gift to say thank-you. He took out a box of chocolates for my mom and dad, and just as he gave them to my mom, my dad opened the front door from work.

He came inside and was happy to see us all. He thanked Ed for the chocolates then went upstairs to change. Ed then turned to me and said, "Here is a little something for you, darling." He took out a little red square box and gave it to me, kissing me first. I hugged him and thanked him then opened the box to reveal a chain with a little gold heart on it. I was so stunned; it was really beautiful. I threw my arms around Ed's neck and kissed him. He said I had a big piece of his heart in my heart. I nearly burst out crying; it was the sweetest thing anyone had said to me. Then Ed opened the chain and put it around my neck. Ross came over and looked at it and said, "Lovely, Mommy." I was ecstatic about this generous gesture of Ed's. My mom admired it, and then I went to arrange my yellow roses in a vase and put them on a table in the lounge. They were such a lovely color, and I would never forget this moment. Here, I had a piece of Ed's heart around my neck. When my dad came downstairs and got something to drink, he joined us in the lounge and said, "Red, you look happy." (Red was my nickname.)

I said, "I am very happy, and look what Ed gave me!" My dad admired it and said it was lovely. We then told my mom and dad that my airfare was fully paid for, and that I was just waiting for my passport, which should arrive that week. Ed asked me if I would wrap the scarf he had bought his mother and the shirt he had bought his sister. I said, of course, and went to get the paper and scissors. Ed helped me wrap, and we found little cards that I had made and put them on the gifts. Ed was delighted with them and put them in his packet to take back to the ship.

I then asked if I had time to bath Ross; he had made the car by now and was talking to his grandpa and showing him how it worked. My mom said yes, and she also asked if I would quickly set the table with Ed. We threw the tablecloth on the table, and I put the mats down. Ed got the cutlery, and we put it out.

I said, "Ross must eat at the big table tonight with us as it was a special occasion as it was Ed's last night with us all." My mom agreed, and Ed brought Ross's high chair through from the kitchen and put it at his seat at the table. We then had to pry Ross away from his Lego car so we could take him for a bath. I put bubbles in the bath for him as Ed took his T-shirt off, and then he got into the bath. He was such a good child; he always listened or nearly always. I let him play for a while with the bubbles, and then we played with him with the bubbles. Ed covered his whole face in bubbles, and Ross laughed so hard my dad even came upstairs to see what was going on, and he also laughed when he saw Ed covered in bubbles. Then he got out, and I dried him and put his pajamas and slippers on him.

We went downstairs to eat and all sat down at the table. My dad poured us all some wine and a little cold drink for Ross in a special glass. Then my dad said he would like to say something, and he said thank-you to Ed for coming into our lives and becoming a part of our family. I was really touched by that, and we all said "Salud" and had a sip of wine. My mom had made a truly South African dish called babootie, which was scrumptious. Ross ate nicely as he knew he was at the big table with us, which was a special occasion.

After dinner, we all sat chatting on the veranda, and my dad asked Ed how long the ship took to get back to Naples, and he made sure Ed would be there in Rome to fetch me from the airport and take me to his home in Naples. Ed said he would be there he had nothing to worry about.

My mom and I went inside to stack the dishwasher and tidied the kitchen. I then said I must go and put Ross to bed as he had school the next day. I went outside and said to Ross it was time for bed; he then kissed everyone, and Ed picked him up and put him on his back to give him a piggyback ride up the stairs to his bedroom. I followed them and thought Ed made Ross so happy and me. We read him a story, and Ed said he would see him in the morning and go to school with him in Grandpa's car. Ross was glad to hear that. He hugged me and then Ed gave him a big hug. We turned the light off, and Ross said, "Night, you two lovebirds." Ed and I looked at each other and burst out laughing; it was so funny for Ross to say that as it was something my mom said, and he had copied her.

Ed and I went downstairs, and my folks were watching a program on TV, so we sat down and watched with them. When it finished, my mom and Dad got up and said they were going to bed, and we must sleep well. I said we would, and if it was okay if we both got a lift into town with my dad in the morning. He said, of course, that was good he would see us in the morning bright and early.

Ed and I turned the TV off, and I put on my favorite CD by Whitney Houston, and we listened to our love song. I got up, and Ed enfolded me in his arms as we danced around the lounge. My heart felt so full and happy to be close to Ed. He whispered in my ear that he wanted to make love to me. I said, "Yes, that would be lovely. Let me switch the music center off, and we can go to my room." Everything seemed so wonderful that evening. It was our last night together; the next time we met, it would be in Italy. I was so fulfilled and happy in Ed's arms.

We walked into my bedroom, and I put my little radio on, and there was some lovely music coming out of it. Ed and I decided to have a shower together. We both got under the shower naked, and the water cascaded over our bodies. We kissed and hugged and washed each other. I then got out, dried myself, and had not taken my heart chain off my body since Ed put it on me. Ed got out as the bathroom was too small for us both to dry each other. I was in my passionate killer nightie by the time Ed opened the bathroom door and came out with the towel around his waist. I looked at him; his black hair was glistening from the water. I could not believe that this good-looking man was about to make love to me; he was such a good man and so good with Ross. It made my heart happy to see them together.

Ed and I made love, and it was beyond anything I had experienced with him before because he was so tender and gentle with me as he knew we would be apart for a while. When we had finished and I lay in his arms, he kissed my forehead and said, "I am going to miss you so much that I will live till I see you get off the airplane in Italy."

I said, "You are so right! I am going to miss you as we all are, including your hero, Ross." I kissed Ed, and he held me close I could feel the beat of his heart next to mine and then I lay in his arms, and we must have fallen asleep like that. I awoke about 5:00 a.m. to the birds tweeting outside. I got up and walked through to the kitchen and switched on the kettle; it was too early to see if Ross was awake. I made us some coffee then took it to Ed; he sat up on one arm, and we drank our coffee. He then took me in his arms, and the passion soared again. We made love slowly and so intimately it was mind-boggling. Then Ed got up and had a shower, and I said I would be back to shower it was 6:00 a.m. and I was going to go and wake Ross. Ed said, "Come shower quickly with me," so I hopped in the shower with him. He washed my hair, and I got out dried myself then put my gown and slippers on brushed, my hair, and went upstairs to Ross.

I was glad I had listened to Ed and had my shower it would speed things up. Ross was awake and just about to get out of bed when I walked in to his room. He said, "Good morning, Mom. Where is Ed?" I said he is in the shower. Ross then said, "I want to go and see him."

I said, "Yes, you can, but first let me change you." I turned to his cupboard and took out shorts and a T-shirt for him. He put his little undies on and then his shorts, and I turned back to the cupboard and got his slops out. When I turned back to Ross, he was struggling to get his T-shirt on. I helped him, and he put his slops on and ran out of the room as fast as he could down the stairs and out the back door to see Ed.

I just stood there and laughed. My mom came through and asked if we had a good night. I said, "Yes, very lovely evening. Thank you." And we walked downstairs together. Ed was dressed by the time Ross burst in on him, and he picked him up and hugged him. I knew he was going to miss him terribly. By the time I got downstairs with my mom, Ed was holding Ross in his arms, standing in the kitchen. My mom said, "This is a lovely sight to see!"

We got into town that morning, and when Ed walked me to my office, he asked if I could come to the ship on Wednesday afternoon at 4:00 p.m. and see him off. I said I would ask to get off at 3:30 p.m. and work my lunch hour today. He said, "Great!" He would phone me later. I said okay, and he kissed me and held me close against his chest. I got out on my floor, and Ed said he would go straight down in the lift and walked back to the ship. I said, "Okay, phone me in an hour." He hugged me, and then the lift doors closed.

Ed was all I could think of when I got into my office, I relived the night before us making love and the feelings between us. I could not wait to see him again and knew I just had to be at the ship to say goodbye on Wednesday. I went to my boss's office and asked him if I could work my lunch hour today so that I could go off at 3:30 p.m. to see Ed off on the ship. He said yes outright, and I hugged him; I was so happy. Zuleika came into the office to give David a message, and we told her Ed was going back to Italy. She asked me how things were going with him, and I told her I was leaving in two weeks' time for Rome. She was delighted for me. I turned and left the office and went back to my office to try and do some work and to wait for Ed to phone. I was ecstatically happy and thought life could not get any better.

On Wednesday, I went to work as usual, and Ross had given me a picture to give to Ed as he had colored it in the night before. I told him I would pass it on to him and give Ed a big hug from him. He looked happy when I left him at school and gave him a big hug. I was so excited I was going to see Ed in the afternoon. My dad said he was very happy that things had turned out so well with Ed and gave me a big hug when he dropped me off in town to go to work.

I went to lunch that day and walked into a shoe shop in the workshop called Mia, as Ed had admired a pair of white leather moccasins, and I bought them for him as I knew his shoe size. I also bought him a lovely T-shirt with "South Africa" on it and a big elephant on the front of it in a light-brown color. I asked the assistant to place the items for me in wrapping paper and paid and left the shop. I went back to work and could hardly wait till 3:30 p.m. to leave and catch a taxi to the ship as it was in the container terminal. When I got out the taxi, I had to catch the bus to the ship and got off the bus, and Ed was waiting at the bottom of the stairs to the ship. I ran into his arms, and he kissed me so hard I lost all my air.

I held him so tight, and he whispered in my ear that he wished we could go and make love. I agreed with him and nodded my head. Then he took my hand and said we had an hour before the ship was leaving. He took me up the gang plank and into the ship, and we went and had some coffee together in the dining room. We were the only ones there. I gave Ed the picture Ross had done for him of an airplane and Mommy getting on it. He laughed till he got tears in his eyes and just hugged me and said, "I will miss you both so much. You are my whole life now!"

I hugged him and was crying as well; although they were tears of joy and sorrow. We sat like that for a while, then I gave him the present I had bought him, and he said I was very naughty. I said, "Yes, I am and so are you for buying me my lovely heart necklace." He opened the package and loved the shoes. He tried them on straight away, and they fitted him perfectly. He loved the T-shirt and said he would think of Ross and I whenever he wore it.

Just then, the captain walked into the dining room and walked up to me and hugged me and said he would like to see my ring and congratulated us on our engagement. He was very happy for us and was glad to know I was flying to see Ed on his leave of two weeks as he had only taken half his leave so that he could save the other two weeks for our honeymoon. I thanked him and hugged him back, and he liked the ring; he said Ed did good. I looked at Ed, and he just looked at us both and shook his head as he knew I loved my ring.

After that, the captain wished me well, and we both knew it would probably be the last time we saw each other as Ed had applied for land duty. He was still waiting to hear from the Durban office of the Mediterranean Shipping Company.

Ed then got up came over to me and hugged me; he kissed me long and hard then got gentler. I held on to him, then he said we should go as he had to go on deck. I walked out with him on deck, and he hugged me once more. He said, "I will see you at Rome airport."

I said, "Great, I can't wait only two weeks to go." Then he kissed me again tenderly, and I turned around and walked down the steps.

He watched me all the way and waved at me when I got to the bottom. I blew him a kiss, and he blew me one then he was gone. I looked around and saw the bus so walked over and got in. There was no use waiting around any longer. As the bus pulled away, I felt a little sad for a minute then thought of flying to Rome, and I perked up.

I caught the taxi back to town and walked around, looking at the shops before I caught the bus back home. I was glad things were moving along.

I had half an hour left before I caught the bus, so I thought I would go and see Fawn and see if my passport with my visa was ready. When I got there, she was surprised to see me. She said, no, it had not come yet, but she was getting some passports back from the embassies tomorrow and would let me know. I l said goodbye and walked to the bus. I got on and sat down, feeling a little lonely without Ed.

Chapter 6

As the days went by without Ed, I was kept busy at work, and Ross was glad to see more of me. I had bought a new suitcase to take to visit Ed, and he had phoned me when the ship got to Cape Town. He sounded well just missed Ross and me a lot. I told him it would not be long now, and we would be together in Italy. He said he couldn't wait to see me again. It had only been three days. He said when the ship reached Naples, he would phone me. I said, "Great, that would be good." I carried on going to work, and that weekend, my dad said have I got enough clothes to take with me. I said, "Yes, I think so." He said the weather should be warm there as it was going into their summer. I said, "Yes, but I will still take one or two jerseys."

My last day at work came, and my boss, David, was very happy for me, and so was Zuleika. I finished work at 4:00 p.m., and they said I could go home; they wished me well and said, "We shall see you in two weeks' time." I left and walked out; my dad had phoned me to say he was leaving town early. Would I like a lift? And I had agreed to meet him at his parking garage. I got out the lift and walked to my dad's car; when I got there, he was waiting. I got in, and we drove home together. It was great not to have to wait for the bus. I was leaving the next day to fly to Rome. My flight was leaving at 5:00 p.m., and my dad said he would take me to the airport with Ross and my mom. I was feeling very excited, as although I had been overseas before, I had never gone on my own. I told my dad I had taken out baggage insurance, and he was glad to hear that as my dad worked with insurance although that was life insurance.

When we got home, I hugged my mom and Ross, and my dad said he would take us out to eat seen as I was leaving the next day. I thought that was a great idea as I had the whole of the next day to pack as we were only leaving for the airport at 2:30 p.m. as I had to be there two hours ahead of leaving. Just then, the phone rang, and it was Ed to say that he was leaving to drive to Rome at 6:00 a.m. the next morning as he would have to sleep over somewhere as it was a long trip. He said he was excited and couldn't wait to see me. I said I was just as excited and then he spoke to Ross for a little while. I know he missed him very much.

After that, we left to go to Mont Marte, a lovely restaurant where we had wine, and my mom and dad had saddle of lamb, and I had a fillet steak, my favorite. Ross had a burger and chips and kept asking was he going to see my airplane tomorrow. We said yes and ate our food. It was a lovely evening, and over coffee, my dad said he was going to give me R500.00 for my trip. I said, "No, you don't have to do that," and he said, yes; it was just a little something for me to have to enjoy myself. I had bought presents for his mom a scarf and his sister a T shirt. I had wrapped them and felt quite chuffed. My dad said I must be very aware when I travelled and hold on to my things and keep my bag close to me when in my seat. I said, "Yes, I would." My mom was happy for me, and I am not sure if Ross truly understood I would be going far away, but we told him I would not be coming home for a while. He said he was a big boy now and would stay with Nanna and Gramps and be good. I said, "Yes, that is what I want you to do." As we left the restaurant that night, I was looking forward to seeing Ed again. He was due to phone me that night at 10:00 p.m., our time.

We got home, and I put Ross to bed. I read him a story and said prayers with him. I said, "You are not going to school in the morning. You are going to be here with Mommy helping her pack her suitcase."

He said, "Yes, I am glad." After that, I hugged him and lay with him for a bit, and in no time, he was asleep. I got up and went downstairs; my folks were watching something on the TV. I sat down, and in no time, the phone rang; it was Ed. I chatted to him, and he said he was leaving in the morning for Rome and would stay over tomorrow night at a bed-and-breakfast place as it was a long way to drive. I told him what time I would be landing, and he said not to worry; he would be there to meet me. I said that will be good. "I look forward to seeing you." Then we spoke a bit more and then said goodbye.

After I put the phone down, I chatted with my mom and dad for a while and then said I was going to bed. I was getting undressed when my mom knocked and came inside. She said she would help me pack in the morning. I said, "Okay thanks," then she hugged me good night.

The next morning, I woke up at about 6:00 a.m. and thought today is the day I fly to Rome to meet Ed and go to Naples with him. I got up and went inside to see if Ross was awake. I looked in the bedroom where he slept, and he was still asleep. I left him sleeping and went downstairs. I put the kettle on then went back and made my bed. I got my suitcase down off the cupboard and put it on the bed. I opened it and thought what clothes to take with me. Ed had said it would be summer on the continent. I went back inside and made myself a cup of coffee. I walked out onto the veranda and sat down and had it. I watched the birds flying around and thought of Ed. After my coffee, I went back inside, then I heard Ross coming down the stairs. I peeped around the wall, and he saw me and threw himself into my arms. I held him close for a while and said, "Did you have a good sleep?" He said yes and told me he was thirsty.

I poured him some orange juice and gave it to him. Then we walked into my bedroom, and I started taking things out of the cupboard and putting them on the bed. I asked Ross's advice on one or two things, and he helped me get some clothes together to pack in my suitcase. After that, we went inside, and I took out some muesli and put some in a bowl for him and me, I put milk on, and he sat down with me at the table and we ate. My mom and Dad came downstairs about 7:00 a.m., and they started to get their breakfast together. I chatted to my dad and told him he must not get back from the office late as we had to leave at 3:30 p.m. as I had to be at the airport two hours before I flew. He said not to worry; he would have me there on time.

After my dad left my mom, Ross and I went to my room, and my mom helped me pack my suitcase. Once that was done, we weighed my suitcase so I could see that I was not overweight. Then my mom said, "Let's go to the shops." She needed to buy some groceries.

I said, "First let me shower and change." I had a shower and got dressed then went upstairs to dress Ross who was playing with his Lego car. My mom was getting ready. Then we left the house, and my mom took me to the Travelex to get my travelers' cheques, and that was sorted out. We went to Pick n Pay, and then she took Ross and I to have something to drink at the coffee shop in Buxton Center. I ordered a cappuccino, and my mom also had one. Ross had a chocolate milkshake. When we finished, it was 11:30 a.m., and we both said we must get home now and go and finish the last of my packing.

We got home, and I took Ross outside to have a play. We played a bit of cricket, and Ross seemed happy. My mom made us some sandwiches and then said Ross and I must come inside and eat. By the time we finished, it was 1:30 p.m., so I said, "I think Ross must have a little lie down." I took him upstairs. I read him a story, and then he fell asleep. I dozed next to him, and then my mom shook me awake and said it was 2:15 p.m. and that I should get ready. I went downstairs to my room and had another shower. I was sweaty from playing cricket with Ross. I finished my shower and got dressed in my jeans and a shirt. I put my denim jacket on as well and my boots. I packed my toiletries for my trip and put them in the suitcase as well as some jewelry in my handbag. I made sure I had my passport, ticket, and traveler's cheques all in my handbag. I then carried my suitcase through to the entrance hall and brought my handbag as well. I got a few vitamins I needed and put them in my big case in a ziplock bag. I felt ready. My mom said, "Have you got everything?"

I said, "I hope so. What I haven't got now is too bad." She had woken Ross, and he was watching something on TV. It was nearly three o'clock and my dad walked in and said, "You look good, Rae. Are you all set to go?" I said yes, and he said, "Well, let's pack the car and leave early. We can have something to drink at the airport."

I said, "That's good with me." We packed the suitcase in the boot of the car and got our handbags and closed up the house. My dad asked if I had my passport and ticket, and I said yes, then we left and got in the car.

When we got to the airport, it was 3:45 p.m., and my flight was leaving at 6:00 p.m. so we had plenty of time. I checked in at the counter, and my suitcase when weighed was under the weight, so I was chuffed. I got my boarding pass, and my dad said, "Let's go and have some coffee in the coffee shop. So we had coffee, and Ross had a mango juice. Before we knew it, it was time for me to go and board at the gate they had told me to so we walked there. My mom said she was going to miss me and so did my dad. Ross was holding my hand, and he said, "Mommy, when are you going to come back?" I told him Nanna would show him on the calendar when she got home. He seemed happy with that answer. I hugged and kissed my mom and dad then picked Ross up and hugged and kissed him. After that, I said I would phone as soon as I landed in Rome. They said not to worry what the time was just to phone. I said I would want not to worry them. Then I hugged Ross again and my dad and turned round and walked through the gate. I waved at them through the glass and walked on to board the airplane.

I had a window seat as I wanted to look out. I put my seat belt on and made myself comfortable. I had to fly to Johannesburg first then wait an hour, then catch a connecting flight to Rome. We took off at exactly 6:00 p.m., and the flight was rather quick to Johannesburg. I got off, and we could wait in a lounge. I looked at the shops and bought myself some coffee. Then before I knew it, I was boarding the flight for Rome. I got on and sat near the window again. The flight was fairly full, although the seat next to me was free. We left just after eight o'clock and were no sooner in the air when they started giving us drinks. After that was food, which was great. We could choose beef or chicken. I chose chicken with vegetables. It was all right; nothing to rave about. Then I watched *Pretty Woman* as it was on. After that, I got up went to the loo and then came back and made myself as comfortable as possible and fell asleep. I woke up when they put the overhead lights on. It said five o' clock on my watch but knew I would have to change my time soon. I went to the loo again and came back to my seat. I sat reading till they brought the coffee and tea around. I had some coffee, and after that, they brought the breakfast. I just had continental, which was a croissant and some yoghurt. I felt so excited to see Ed. The voice came over the loud speaker and said we would be landing in half an hour. I could not wait to get off the airplane.

Eventually, we landed, and I got my handbag and followed everyone through to where our luggage came out. I stood waiting and looking around me.

It was a big airport. I got my luggage, then we went through customs, and that was a breeze. I got through that, and the next thing was waiting where everyone waited to be collected. All of a sudden, I saw Ed standing and waving at me. I walked over to him, and he hugged and kissed me. He said, "It is so good to see you. How was your flight?"

I said, "It was okay. Everything went smoothly." He said we were going to leave straight away and drive to a place where we could spend the night as he was sure I was a bit tired. I said not really as I had slept fairly well. I said could we just find a phone so I could phone home. He said "Sure," so we went and phoned. My mom answered the phone and was happy to hear my voice. I told her I was fine and that Ed had fetched me and we were about to leave for Naples. She told me to have a good time, and I asked her to give Ross a big hug from me. She said she would do that, and we hung up.

Ed took me to his car and we drove off as he wanted to show me the Colosseum, so we went there first. It was huge, and we walked around for a while, and then Ed took me for a cup of coffee. Rome was so busy; the traffic was horrendous, and we eventually left and drove out of the city. I was glad to get away from the traffic; we drove for about two hours, then Ed asked me if I was hungry, and I said yes. He stopped at a small café, and we got out and shared a pizza and had something to drink. Then I went to the loo, and we got back in the car and drove for another three hours. By then, I was feeling tired, and Ed said we are nearly there. We stopped at a little bed-and-breakfast called Marcos about six hours away from Naples. We got out, and Ed took my suitcase and a smaller bag he had brought with him. We checked in as Ed had booked ahead as he had stayed here the night before on the way up to Rome to fetch me.

We got to our room, and Ed said, "You want to take a shower?" And I said yes, so I had a shower then got out, and him and I made love.

Then I fell asleep in his arms. It felt so good to be with him. I woke up about two hours later, and Ed said the time was seven o'clock. "Maybe we should go and get something to eat in the village." The B&B only served breakfast. I got up and got dressed, and Ed showered and also changed. We went out to the village, and there were only two restaurants to choose from. We chose the one that was not too busy. Ed found us a corner table, and we ordered a glass of red wine. He said, "Salud, it is great to see you in my country." I had a sip, and we held hands. I said it is lovely to be here. Then I ordered a pasta and so did Ed; they both had seafood in them. We ate when it arrived, as I was hungry and so was Ed. Then we got up and took a walk around the little village. Ed asked how Ross was and my folks, and I said that everyone sent their love. Then we spoke about seeing his mom and sister, and he said they were looking forward to meeting me. He said after breakfast that we would leave, and I agreed. Then we went back to the B&B and fell asleep in each other's arms.

The next morning, we got up, and I had another shower and got dressed; the weather looked like it was going to be another warm day. Ed got up and made us some coffee, and then he had a shower and got dressed. We packed the car then went inside to have some breakfast. It was a lovely breakfast; you could help yourself. The only thing they made was omelets or eggs for you. I ordered a mushroom omelet and had some bacon. Ed had eggs with bacon and tomato. We both had some coffee then got up, and Ed settled the bill, and I went to the bathroom as knew we would be driving for at least three hours. We left at 9:30 a.m. and drove all the way through little villages. After we had been driving and chatting about our wedding, I asked Ed if he had heard from MSC about the job on land he had applied for in Durban. He said he should hear something soon, but nothing had come through yet.

We stopped at about 1:00 p.m. for some lunch; it was just a roll with salami and salad on, which was delicious, and we took our cold drinks with us in the car because we just wanted to reach Naples now. Ed filled the car up with petrol, and we left again at 2:00 p.m. We got to where Ed lived in Arenella in the province of Syracuse at 4:30 p.m., and I had enough driving; it looked lovely with the beach on the one side. He drove me through the town that looked poor, and we stopped in front of his mother's house. We both got out, and Ed took my hand, and we walked inside to meet his mom and sister. His mom was a lot older than I thought, and his sister seemed friendly, although she could not speak much English. Ed went out to get my suitcase and his bag out the car. His mom could speak a little English, and she spoke to me about my trip and my family, and I told her about Ross. She said that Ed had said he was a lovely little boy. I said yes he was and showed her a photo of him, which I carried in my handbag.

Ed gave me room as he was sleeping on the couch as there were only three bedrooms. It was a smallish house and very lived in. We were very tired after our trip, but his mom said we could eat early and go to bed as she could see we were tired. We chatted a bit more with her, then Ed said if I wanted to shower, I could so I got up and went through to my room and unpacked my suitcase a bit and hung up what I could in the small cupboard. I went and had a shower and just put on my tracksuit as I knew after supper I would be hitting the bed.

I came through after my shower, and Ed poured us all a drink I had some wine and so did he. He had also showered as he had done all the driving and was tired. We sat chatting, then we had supper, which was very tasty and sat around the table having some ginger tea. Then I excused myself as was very tired, and Ed said no problem; he had decided to sleep in his sister's room as they had a fold-out bed.

So he and I said good night and went to our rooms. He kissed me good night in my bedroom and said he would miss holding me. I agreed with him and went to brush my teeth. I no sooner hit the pillow and was asleep.

The next morning, I woke up and went to the loo. The house was very quiet. Then when I got into bed, I heard a little knock at the door; it was Ed standing there with a cup of coffee for both of us. He sat on my bed, and we drank the coffee. He hugged me and said, "Do you want to go to the beach today?"

I said, "Yes, that would be lovely. You can show me around."

He said he had slept well and felt refreshed. I also said I slept well. Then I got up and put my gown on. I felt I had better behave well here as it was his mom's home. Ed had put a T-shirt on, and we went out to the kitchen. His mom was up, and she said good morning to us both and asked me if I wanted an egg for breakfast with toast. I said I would just have toast as I did not feel very hungry. Then Ed brought the toast to the table, and I had two slices with more coffee. His sister had left for work already so we sat chatting with his mom. She was a lovely lady, and I liked her, although I could see she really loved having Ed around. That was a good thing, though. Then Ed said, "Let's go and get our costumes on and go to the beach." So I got up and went and changed. I made my bed and put on some sunblock.

We walked to the beach as it was not a long way away. The beach was quite small, but the sand was soft, and the water was crystal clear. Ed and I had a swim and sat in the sun on our towels. We chatted and had the bottled water he had brought with from home. It was great to just be together. We chatted about our wedding and Ross and getting a place to live in. We decided that if Ed's transfer came through soon, then we would find a place together and move in. Then we could settle ourselves and get Ross to come and live with us too. We got up and had another swim, then Ed said he was feeling hungry; we must go back to his mom's house. So we did we took a leisurely walk back, and I could feel I had been in the sun. Luckily, we both had sunblock on and had gone a sort of golden brown color. I had a shower when we got in and so did Ed. His mother had been knitting and had also been cooking some pasta for dinner. It smelt delicious.

Ed made us each a sandwich as his mom had her lunch already. We sat in the lounge talking with her, and Ed said he wanted her and his sister Georgia to be at the wedding; he told his mom he would pay for her air ticket. His mom smiled, and they spoke in Italian for a while. Later on, his mom turned to me and smiled and said that although they were Catholics, she did not mind if I was not as they were not very religious. I thanked her, and she told Ed and I that the next day they were having his aunt and cousins to visit for lunch, and we must be here so they could meet me. Ed said yes, we would be, and then he got up, took my hand, and pulled me outside. He then kissed me and said it was terrible not being able to sleep with me when I was so close by. I said it will not be for long; he said no. This weekend, he was going to take me into Naples to a small place where we could spend the night on Saturday evening. I said that will be lovely, as he said it was small at his mom's house. I said if you want to do that, it is all right with me.

The next day for lunch, there were quite a few people all in this little house. There was Ed's mom's sister and her two children one boy and a girl. Then there was his uncle on his dad's side with his wife and two boys. We all had something to drink, and everyone was talking in Italian. Ed introduced me to everyone; the children were young teenagers, so they stood around, chatting and laughing. I felt a bit odd as I could not speak Italian very well, but Ed was very good and hardly left my side. We all sat down at a big table outside to have our lunch. There were salads and cold meat and delicious homemade bread. It really was a delicious meal. Then Ed's mom brought out gelato and sorbet, and that really was to die for. We all ate well, and I could understand Italian a lot better than I thought I would. His sister had taken the day off, and Georgia sat near us, and I felt that I really got to know her as we chatted in Italian and English. After that lunch, everyone said their goodbyes, and Ed said, "Come, we will go and lie down in your room." So we did, and in no time, we were asleep. It had all been a lot for us to deal with.

I woke up and looked at the time, and it was 5:00 p.m. Ed stirred next to me and got up to make us a cup of tea. I went through to the kitchen with him. His mom and Georgia had tidied up the table outside and cleaned the kitchen. I told him I should have helped, and he said that I was the guest in the house. We sat outside at the big table and had our tea. Ed asked if I wanted to go dancing that night as it was a Friday night. I said, "Yes, that will be lovely." I asked if Georgia was going to join us. He said he would ask her if she wanted to or not. We sat chatting, then his mom and Georgia came through and joined us. We all spoke in English, so I could understand and his mom said his aunt and uncle were happy for both of us, just sorry that they would not be at the wedding. Ed said, "We are going to get a video done of the wedding so they could always watch it when you bring it back." His mom agreed. We asked Georgia if she wanted to come out with us, and she said her boyfriend was coming to fetch her soon to go out to dinner, and she and him would meet us later at the disco. We both said okay and then his mom asked us if we were going to eat with her; we said yes we would, as we were in no rush to go out early.

I asked Ed if I could iron some pants and a shirt I wanted to wear, and he said yes and showed me where I could iron them. After that, I got changed, and we went and had a drink with his mom and Georgia, whose boyfriend, Marco, had arrived. Marco ran a restaurant not far from where they lived in the village. He could only speak Italian, so I tried hard to speak to him in Italian. Ed helped me, and then Georgia and Marco left to go out. Ed and I set the table and then his mom dished us up some scrumptious spaghetti bolognaise she had made for us. It really was scrumptious, and then Ed and I chatted with her and then Ed told her that tomorrow we were going to go away for the night. She said that was good and that we must do our thing. Then Ed let me phone home, and I spoke to Ross and my mom and they all seemed well. I told her we were having a good time; she said we must enjoy ourselves as it wouldn't be long, and I would be flying back home again.

After that, it was about 9:00 p.m. when Ed and I went out to the disco, which was nearby in the village. When we got there, the music was pulsating, and the dance floor was full. We sat down for a while, and the next minute, Ed saw a friend who joined us and I remembered him from the ship. He was with his girlfriend, and we then got up and danced for a while. The music was great, and then we came back and saw that Georgia and Marco had joined our table. We ordered drinks and tried to talk, but the music was too loud. We just got up and went and danced again. Ed told me that he was going to ask his friend Paulo to be his best man. I said I had not met him yet, and he said that tomorrow I would meet him. We had a good time, and then at 1:00 a.m., we decided to go back home. By then, we had danced ourselves out and were tired. Ed drove back, and we were home in no time; he kissed and hugged me at the door to my room and whispered that soon we would be together close up again. I agreed and then went into my room and changed. My clothes smelled of smoke, so I put them to one side. I got into my pajamas and fell into bed. I slept so well that I didn't wake up until 9:00 a.m. when Ed brought me a cup of coffee. It was an overcast day, and he said we should just get up have some breakfast then leave as he wanted to show me some sites along the coast. I said sure I would get up and shower then get dressed.

We said goodbye to his mom, and Ed drove me along the Amalfi Drive, which was breathtaking. We stopped at a lovely little restaurant and had some lunch. The view was truly lovely with the sea for miles, and we sat chatting about where we would like to go for our honeymoon. Ed took my hand and kissed my ring.

He said, "I can't wait to be married to you." Then we paid the bill and left. He said we were going to stay at a lovely place called Hotel Onde Verde, and as we drove in, the man came out the hotel to tell us where to park. Ed carried our bags into the hotel where another man took them from him. They then showed us our room, which had a stunning sea view. Ed said should we go for a walk down to the beach as it was not a long way.

I said, "Yes, that would be lovely." We changed into shorts and slops, and Ed hugged me before we left. We walked out the hotel hand in hand. It was a gray-looking day, and we walked for quite a while along the beach. I was looking for shells, but there weren't very many. We came back to the hotel, and Ed took me to the veranda where we ordered coffee and cake. Ed loved chocolate cake, so we shared a piece; it was huge, and then Ed said, "Should we have a late supper?" I said that was okay with me. We went and asked what time was the latest we could eat, and they said 8:00 p.m. So we walked back to our room. We had a Jacuzzi, so we put bubbles in the water and had a luxurious time. Eventually, Ed was getting all amorous, so we got out and went inside and made love on the bed. It was lovely to fall asleep in Ed's arms. When I woke up, it was 7:00 p.m., so I got up, showered, and dressed in my dress I had brought with me. Ed was in the shower and seemed happy, humming a tune to himself. He got out the shower and hugged me and told me how much he loved me and that it was great being with me in his hometown. I said I was having a great time and loved being with him. He said next Saturday, we would be saying goodbye at the airport, and I said, "You are quite right." I asked him when he thought he would hear if he was going to be given an office job in Durban at MSC. He said he hoped he would hear this coming week as he needed to know what was going to happen. I said, "Don't worry. We will sort it out. Let's just take one step at a time." Then he got dressed, and we walked down to dinner.

When we got there, there was lovely music playing, and some people were dancing on the dance floor. We ordered our starter then got up and had a dance. Ed held me close and whispered, "It is so good to have you here." I agreed then we went to eat. The hotel really was great, and after our main course, we danced, and Ed really enjoyed himself as did I. We eventually had our pudding and some coffee, then Ed said, "Do you feel like strolling outside?"

I said okay, and it was great just being together. After that, we went to our room, and Ed started to peel my dress off me. I did not complain as I wanted him as much as he wanted me. We made passionate love again, and then I must have fallen asleep in his arms. I woke the next morning with Ed looking at me sleeping. I hugged him, and he got up and the next thing, there was a knock at the door, and Ed put one of the hotel gowns on and opened the door. They had brought us a pot of hot coffee. Ed thanked them and poured me a cup. He brought it to me in bed, and I thought I could really get used to being this spoilt. Ed then said we would have to get up and get dressed as we had to be out the rooms by 10:00 a.m., and it was 8:45 a.m. I eventually hugged Ed, and we kissed, then he said, "Let's go and have our last Jacuzzi for a while." So I got up, and within minutes, we were in the Jacuzzi. It was great, and we both got out, showered, and I quickly dried my hair with the hairdryer they supplied in the rooms. I got dressed, and we left at 9:45 a.m. We went downstairs, and Ed paid the bill. They offered us breakfast, which we took them up on as it was included. We sat in the lovely breakfast room overlooking the sea and ate and chatted. I could not believe that next Sunday I would be back in South Africa. Ed said he would miss me, and until he knew what was happening with him being moved, he would have to wait and see where things took him.

We drove back to his mom's house, and it took us till 4:00 p.m. as we took a leisurely drive and Ed apologized for not being able to take me to Sorrento, but I said I am sure we will come again another day. He said if I wanted to go, he would phone his mom, but I said no as there was not much time left to spend with her, and so we carried on driving. By the time we got back, his mom had made us a lovely supper of tagliatelle Alfredo, which we had later and a good bottle of red wine. It was delicious, and then I said I was tired and excused myself and went to bed. Ed kissed me good night and said he would miss me. I said, "So would I."

When I woke up the next morning, Ed brought me coffee in bed and said, "How about we take Mom shopping in the village?" I said that was a great idea, so I got up showered and got dressed. It was a lovely sunny day. I went to have breakfast, and his mom was there, busy, getting her basket together and her shopping list. I finished my breakfast, and Ed got the car out and then we drove to the village. His mom said that tomorrow we were going to visit her sister as she had asked us to come for lunch. I said that would be nice, and we bought the foodstuff she wanted. Then I went into a clothes shop and saw a lovely T-shirt, which I bought. It had Italy on the front, and I thought it was most appropriate. After that, Ed took me into a little toy shop, and I bought Ross a Lego set. Ed also bought him an English book on ships. After that, we took his mom to a little coffee shop and had some lunch; it was a lovely morning. Ed drove us home and asked me if I wanted to go for a walk along the beach. His mom went to lie down as she was tired after shopping.

Ed and I walked along the beach holding hands, and I had never been happier. As we walked back to his mom's house, he said he wished he would hear from his work regarding his job. As we got back, he put the kettle on for some tea, and the phone rang. He answered it in Italian and then spoke a while. After he got off the phone, he said it was his company and that the job in Durban in the office had come through, and he was to start there in two weeks' time. I said, "That is wonderful! Are you happy?" He said he was ecstatic. His mom came through, and we told her the good news. She was very happy for Ed and hugged him. He said he would leave on the ship next Wednesday and be in South Africa on the Friday so he could start his office job on the Monday. I was so delighted for Ed; everything was coming together now. He said we would leave early on Friday morning to drive back to Rome as I had to catch the flight to South Africa on the Saturday. I agreed with him, and we spent the rest of the week with his mom. Ed and I took her to Naples, and she found a lovely outfit for the wedding. She seemed happy about that. I bought my mom a scarf and my dad a blue shirt, his favorite color. Other than that, I was ready to leave as I had met his mom and sister Georgia now, and they both seemed like a lovely people.

As I kissed Ed's mom goodbye on the Friday morning, she hugged me and said we would meet at the wedding in December. I said, "Yes, not long to go now." It was already the end of May, and I had lots to get organized. Ed got in the car, and we drove off. We chatted along the way, and Ed said he was looking forward to his new job. It was going to be so different to what he was used to. He said he was going to be trained in exporting and importing and could eventually become the manager of that division. I said that would be lovely, and he should try and do that. He agreed with me. I said, "Where will you stay?" And he said he would have to find a place when he got back. I said I would look out for a place for him. We stopped at the same bed-and-breakfast as before and just had supper and fell into bed. In the morning, Ed made love to me, and we had a shower together. I would not see him for six days, then we would be together and he would be off the ship. I said maybe you should come and stay with us for a while till you find a place. I will speak with my folks. He said, "Okay, that would be great." Then we went to breakfast and left after that for Rome.

The scenery was lovely driving to Rome, and we stopped near the city and had lunch and looked at some of the shops. Ed bought me a lovely chain bracelet with a butterfly on it in silver. He put it on my arm, and it looked great. I bought him a lovely silver pen for his new job, and he loved it. After that, we drove straight to the airport and had a cup of coffee once my cases had gone through. I held his hand and said, "I could not wait for you to be back in South Africa with me." He agreed with me and said our lives were only just starting together. He walked me to the gate and hugged and kissed me and thanked me for coming. I said I had a lovely time, and he kissed me again and held my face in his hands. I then had to walk through, and once I got on the other side of the glass, I blew him kisses. He blew me some back. I walked through to go to customs and got through that then walked around the shops and waited for my flight to be called. I was looking forward to seeing my folks and Ross again. I had a great time with Ed and his family but knew my home was back in South Africa.

Chapter 7

As I got off the plane in Johannesburg, I could not wait to board the plane to Durban. I had to collect my luggage and go through customs, which went smoothly. I bought myself a Coke and sat reading a magazine near my gate as I had my boarding pass and had checked in already. I just wanted to get home to my son and my folks. As soon as my flight was called, I was in the queue and was the first one on the plane. I got a window seat and sat down. It was Sunday morning, and I could hardly believe I was back in South Africa.

As we landed at Durban Airport, I was so relieved to be back on South African soil I got my bag and was off the flight, first one down the stairs. I got to the carousel that held our big cases, and as I got there, they started coming out. I did not have to wait long and then I saw my suitcase and took it off the roundabout and put it on the trolley. Then I pushed the trolley out through the doors and saw Ross; straight away, he came running to me, and I went down and caught him in my arms. I was so happy to see him. I hugged and kissed him and held him close. Then I saw my mom and dad and hugged and kissed them both. My dad pushed my trolley to the car, and we got in and drove home.

When we got home, I opened my case and took out the Lego airplane I had bought for Ross and the T-shirt Ed had bought him and gave it to him. He was delighted and started to build the Lego airplane straight away. I gave my folks what I had bought them, and my mom loved her scarf, and my dad liked his shirt. It was so good to be home. Then the tiredness hit me and my mom said I must go and have a sleep after I had lunch. I did go and lie down with Ross beside me on my bed; it felt good to be in my bed.

When I woke up, I asked my mom if I could please phone Ed to tell him I was back home and everything was good. They said yes, and I told them that Ed's land job had come through with the Mediterranean Shipping Company and that he would be back in Durban on Friday as he was leaving Naples on Wednesday. They were very happy for Ed and I, and my mom and dad both said things were falling into place well for us. I asked them if Ed could stay with us while we looked for a place to live in, and they agreed.

I spoke to Ed and told him he could stay with us and go to work with Ross, my dad and I every day, and he was delighted. It was so good to hear his voice, and I was glad he was coming home on Friday. I looked at SA as his home now. He had left Naples behind. Yes, his mom lived there, but he and I and Ross were going to be making a home for ourselves now.

I went back to work the next day after a good night's sleep and felt refreshed and rested. Everyone wanted to know how my trip had gone, and I told them over a cup of coffee so I would not have to repeat myself. They were very happy for me. I told David, my boss, that Ed had gotten a land job with his company and was starting on the Monday, and he was very happy everything was happening for us. I asked him if he knew of any granny flats in Durban North as he lived there, and he said he would keep his ears open for us.

Ed phoned me on the Tuesday night to let me know he was packed and looking forward to seeing Ross and I again on the Friday. He was just getting a lift back to South Africa on the ship to save the company paying for an airfare, and he could bring an extra case as he had to wear smart clothes like a suit and tie now that he was going to be working in the office. He said he had bought five new shirts for his work and would show me when he arrived.

Suddenly, I thought when I got off the phone, *Where is Ed going to put his clothes?* My mom said she would make space for him to hang his clothes in Ross's cupboard as Ross did not have a lot of hanging clothes. I said that is a good idea, and I made some space in my cupboard for him to put his undies and T-shirts. I was so excited to see him again and to start our lives together, looking for a place to make into our home.

The next day, I went to work, and David, my boss, said there was a granny flat going in the road behind where he lived, and he knew the people. I said, "Great! Could we look at it on the Saturday?" And he said he would phone the people straight away and set it up. He said they had a lovely garden and a big swimming pool. I said it sounded unreal!

On Friday, I worked my lunch hour so that I could leave an hour early to go and meet Ed at the ship. My mom and Ross picked me up at 3:30 p.m., and I was waiting outside the building where I worked. I got in and kissed and hugged Ross, and my mom drove us down to the terminal where the ship was. We all got out with Ross and walked to the ship. Ed saw us and ran down the steps and picked Ross up in his arms and swung him around. Ross was giggling, and I just smiled then he came and hugged and kissed me. He hugged and kissed my mom and then said we must come on board to help him carry his things. I said okay and we walked up the stairs on board. We walked to his cabin, and he had two suitcases and a bag. I carried the bag, and he gave my mom a big packet and Ross a smaller packet then he walked out carrying both suitcases. The captain met us and shook hands and hugged Ed and said they were going to miss him. I said now I have him, and he smiled and agreed with me and said I must look after him. I said I would.

He said Ed must stay in touch with him, and Ed had his address and telephone number. Then we turned and walked down the stairs and turned and waved goodbye to him. We walked to the car, and Ed had tears in his eyes as he had been working with the captain since he started on board this ship six years ago. So he was going to miss him a lot.

We got home, and Ed walked inside, and I hugged him and said, "Welcome to your South African home for now!" He looked at me, smiled, kissed, and hugged me. Ross was delighted to show Ed where he could hang his clothes, and Ed just smiled and thanked us for everything. We unpacked his suitcases and fitted everything in the cupboards and then went to sit on the veranda and have a drink.

I told Ed that my boss had a granny flat one road away from where he lived for us to look at, and he was blown away and so excited. I said we were going to go tomorrow morning my folks were going to take us to have a look. As they also wanted to see where there grandson would be staying. It had two bedrooms and a little lounge and kitchen and a car port. We chatted about it for a while, and Ed said we could move at the end of the month if we liked it. I said that would be great as it would give us time to buy some furniture. He agreed. We only had five months to go till our wedding, and my dress was being made. I had chosen the material that week with my mom.

My older sister Allison would be flying out from Australia at the beginning of December as we were getting married on December

5, 1986, the day after my dad's birthday on December 4, 1986. I could not have been happier. My other sister, Sandy, who lived in Johannesburg with her husband and two sons was coming down at the end of the month to choose bridesmaid dresses and shoes as there was not a lot of time left. We had decided Ross was going to wear white satin three-quarter pants and a white long-sleeve shirt with a blue bow tie and blue socks and white pumps. He liked the idea, and he would carry a white heart satin pillow with the rings tied on with blue ribbons.

As we drove to the granny flat the next day, we were all looking forward to seeing it. We got there and met the man; his name was Greg, and his wife's name was Jill. They showed us the place, and we fell in love with it. It was just what we wanted and had a lovely big garden and pool for all of us to have fun in. We asked if we could move in at the end of the month, and they said no problem. They said they would draw up the lease for us to sign, and we would have to put a full month's deposit down, and Ed agreed to that without a problem. I was ecstatic when we left, and Ross said he liked the place plus Greg and Jill had a lovely spaniel dog called Rufus. Ross, of course, liked the dog. I was delighted and Ed said he was chuffed that was one big thing taken care of. Now he had to look for a good second-hand car as we could not move in without having a car; otherwise, how would we get to work and Ross to school. I agreed and said, "Let's just take one thing at a time." Ed agreed with me, and then my dad took us for lunch at the Country Club golf course. We had a buffet lunch, and it was delicious. We were all so happy, and my folks both said they liked the granny flat, and it was close to them and the shops and not too far to work and Ross's school.

The first night Ed slept with me in our home, I lit all the candles, and he opened a bottle of champagne he had bought to celebrate us finding our new home.

I put on a passion-killer nightdress, and he poured us each a glass and we listened to some classical music. I had never felt so happy as I felt as Ed held me in his arms and caressed my shoulders and slowly began kissing my neck and lips. Then he made love to me, and we both felt so at peace and satisfied as I lay in his arms and fell asleep. He whispered in my ears, "Amore!"

When we woke up the next morning, I got up and went to make coffee for us. As I turned to go up the stairs to see if Ross was awake, he came bounding down the stairs and threw himself into my arms. I hugged him and asked him if he wanted to come and have tea and biscuits with Ed and I in bed. He said yes, then I put him down and he went running into my bedroom to see Ed. I made the coffee, tea, and biscuits and took it through to our room on a tray. We all sat there eating and dipping our biscuits. I thought this is it! The two most favorite men in my life in my bed life could not get better. Ed then said, "How about we go down for a walk along the beach then have breakfast?"

I said, "That is an awesome idea. Let's do it."

Then he said after breakfast, "We can go looking at some furniture for our new place."

I said, "Yes, you are on." I took Ross's hand and took him upstairs to his bedroom for him to change. I made his bed, then my mom popped her head around the corner, and I told her what we would be doing, and she said that was great. She was on her way to church, and we hugged goodbye.

I went downstairs and showered and changed into jeans and a long-sleeve T-shirt. Then Ed showered and also changed into jeans. He hugged me and said, "I am so happy I have everything I ever wanted," and with that, Ross ran into the room and Ed picked him up and held him in his arms.

We had a group hug, then we left. Ed had hired a car and we got in it. It was a blue-colored Clio, and we drove down to the beach. We got out, and Ed put Ross on his shoulders and took my hand as we walked along past the lighthouse, then Ed put Ross down and he said, "You two have made me the happiest man in the world."

I said, "Great, but I am hungry now. Could we please go and eat?"

He said, "Okay, let's go to Lara's at the Buxton Center." So we drove up there and got a table and ordered our coffee a milkshake for Ross and some breakfast.

After that, we drove to Springfield Park and went to Makro to look at some furniture. We never really saw anything great, so we came out and went into a bed shop. We found a double bed we liked and then we looked at a bed for Ross. We found one in the shape of a car, and Ross just loved it. Ed bought them both, and we asked to have them delivered at the end of the month to our new address.

After that, we drove home, and all played soccer in the garden with Ross. My folks were home, and my dad was making a *potjie* for lunch. Ed had never tasted potjie food, and he said he was looking forward to it. My dad offered Ed a beer, and he poured me a glass of wine. Ross had some juice, and my mom and I made some rice and a salad. I set the table, and then we were ready to eat. The potjie was chicken and prawn, and Ed said it was delicious. We all ate, and Ross could not finish his food he was looking tired. I took him upstairs to his bed and put him down to sleep.

I came downstairs, and Ed said he would like to ask us something. We said what, and he said he would like to adopt Ross before we got married so that we could all have the same surname. I said that was a great idea; we must get hold of a lawyer.

My mom said she knew of a lawyer friend called Brian; she would phone him and speak to him tomorrow. I said "Great," and

Ed smiled and said it would help a lot if she would do that for us. I was feeling so happy and at peace with everything. I helped my mom clear up and did the dishes. My mom and dad went to lie down. Ed came up to me and put his arms around me and asked if he could phone his mom to say he was safely here and starting work tomorrow. I said that would be fine, so he phoned her and I said hello to her, and she sounded happy for the two of us. We told her that we had found a place to live, and she was delighted for us. Ed told her about Ross, and she said she looked forward to meeting him as she had only seen photos of him. We then went to have a lie down, and as I lay in Ed's arms, I thought we are going to have a great life together forever. I then fell asleep.

The next day, we all got up early, and Ed took the hired car back and got in our car, and we took Ross to school first and, Ed had to come into school with us and then we my dad drove Ed and I into town. We got out near my building, and I walked Ed down to Field Street to the Mediterranean Shipping Company building and said goodbye to him by the lifts. He said he would phone me later in the morning so we could meet for lunch. I then walked to my building and went into the office. I felt so complete as a person and had never been happier.

At ten o'clock, I was having a cup of coffee when Ed phoned, and I asked him how things were going, and he said he was enjoying himself and if we could meet at 1:00 p.m. for lunch. I said, "Yes, why don't you walk to my building, and then we can walk to the Albany for lunch."

He said, "Great idea and I have good news for you."

I said, "I can't wait to hear it."

I met Ed at 1:00 p.m., and he said that some money was being paid to him from a safety fund when he was on the ship, and he would be able to buy his car with it. I said, "Great, that is awesome news."

Then he said my mom had phoned him, and it was straightforward. To adopt Ross, we just had to supply our ID books, and they were going to draw up the adoption papers, and they would be ready by this Friday, and we just had to sign them. I hugged him and said, "You are a one-in-a-million man."

He smiled at me and said it would make him so happy to have such a special child as my son his son also. I looked at him with tears in my eyes, and he got up and hugged me. Then we walked back to my office, and he saw me inside and then left to walk back to his. He said, "I will meet you outside your office to catch the bus home at 5:00 p.m."

And I said, "Yes, see you then."

At 5:00 p.m., I met Ed, and he was holding a bunch of yellow roses—my favorites. He gave them to me and said I was giving him a gift by sharing Ross with him and making it official. I hugged him, and we walked to the bus. He said, "Soon we won't be catching this bus. I will have my own car." He spoke about the work he was doing and said he felt he would enjoy it. He said it was a little different to working on a ship and would take a while to get used to it, but he felt he could do well at it.

We got home and said hello to Ross and my mom, and then Ed and I went and had a shower together. I got into my tracksuit and went to make Ross dinner. I took him for a bath, and he played with his toys in the bath. Ed came in and said, "Would you like me to be your dad?" Ross's face lit up, and he smiled and said yes; he would like that as he loves him. I turned around as I got tears in my eyes. Ed saw and hugged me. He said, "By the end of the week on Friday, Ross could call me dad."

Ross said, "I want to call you dad now!"

Ed was so surprised he had tears and hugged Ross and said, "You have a deal, buddy," and gave him a high-five. Ross got his pajamas on, and we took him downstairs to eat. Just then, my dad walked in and said hello to us all. He poured us all a drink, and Ross ate his dinner. He had to get to sleep early as we got up earlier now to leave for work and school as we had Ed to come with us. After that, I gave him a little ice cream, and Ed helped him eat it. Then Ed put him on his back and gave him a piggyback ride up the stairs to his bed. I read him a story, then he wanted Ed to read, so he did, then we hugged and kissed, and I lay there for a while with him as Ed sat on the bed, and he fell asleep.

Ed put his arm around me and walked downstairs to go and have dinner with the folks. We sat at the table and told my dad that Ed was adopting Ross and that it was a straightforward process. He said he was very happy for us all and was glad everything was working out for us all. Ed told my folks about the fund that was paying him out this money so he was going to buy a new car. Ed and I had spoken about it and thought about getting a RAV.

Then all of a sudden, out of the blue, my aunty Joan phoned and said she was selling her white Honda Ballade. Ed and I went to look at it, and Ed bought it straight away. We drove back to Durban in it and only had two weeks to go till we moved in. We were looking forward to it. Things were going well with Ed at work, and I was working hard and saving for the wedding. My dress was cut out already, and I was going for my first fitting that week. All was working out according to plan. One lunch hour, Ed and I went shopping at Sheet Street for linen for our new place and got everything and had to lug it back on the bus. Ed was getting tired of the bus, but it saved paying for parking, and while we were saving for the wedding and until we moved, we would have to stick to it.

Chapter 8

All of a sudden, it was the day we were moving, and Ed and I had packed our things and Ross's things. The adoption had gone through the day before, and we had celebrated by going out to Le Monte Marte Restaurant for dinner. Ross and Ed were inseparable. It was great to see, and I was very happy for them. Ed drove Ross and I across to the new place after we had packed the car to capacity. Ross was so excited, and Ed said he was going to buy Ross a dog as soon as we were settled. I was left there with Ross and my mom; first the beds arrived and were put in the bedrooms, then my mom and I made them with the new linen we had washed to make it soft. Then our lounge suite arrived, and then Ed came back with the TV and music center. He connected that with his new friend from work Marco.

Then my mom went out and bought some rolls, cheese and ham, and came back and made lunch for us all. My dad had gone to play golf. We made tea and ate lunch outside on our veranda as it was a warm day. Then after lunch, my mom left, and I thanked her for her help. She said the house was going to be so quiet without us. I said she would get used to it eventually.

Then once the TV was working and Ross was watching Walt Disney, we had a drink on the veranda with Marco. His girlfriend from Naples was flying out for our wedding. Ed had asked Marco to be his best man. He had agreed, and we all sat talking about work the wedding and life in general. Marco said he was thinking of proposing to Isabella when she came out for the wedding, and Ed said he should go for it. Look how happy we were. He said he would think about it some more.

Once Marco left, I made Ed, Ross, and I some hamburgers and chips, and we sat outside eating them. Ross said, "I like our new home, Mom and Dad." It nearly got me crying to hear him say "Dad." After that, we watched a movie on mnet then put Ross to bed after we had read him a story. His bedroom was done out in cars, and he liked his new bed.

Then Ed and I made some coffee and took it to our bedroom once we had locked up. Ed took me in his arms and said, "Now I have everything I ever wanted. I just have to make you my wife and it will be complete."

I said, "Yes, you are right." Then I lit some candles, and Ed and I made love on our new bed. So we had christened it now.

On the Monday, Ed drove us to work and Ross to school. All went well, and we had found a parking garage in town that did not rip us off. We parked, then Ed held my hand as we walked to work together. He looked at me and said, "Who would have thought this is where we would be six months ago?" I agreed with him; he kissed me goodbye at my building then walked to his office.

I was so happy and felt we had achieved so much in the last few months. I went for a fitting for my wedding dress after work, and Ross and Ed waited outside for me. I was adamant he could not see me before the big day. The invitations had been posted, and we had already had some replies, all in favor of coming to the big day. It was getting exciting now. Ed had picked a place for our honeymoon but would not tell me; he said it was a surprise.

Life went on smoothly, and soon, it was the big day and I went to sleep at my mom's the night before so that we could make it special. Ross came with me, and Ed said, "You are going to leave me alone." His mom and sister were out and were staying at a B&B down the road from us in Durban North. I said, "Yes, it is only for one night," and then Ross was going to be staying with his Nan and Gramps while Ed and I were on honeymoon.

All of a sudden, my hair and nails were done, and my dress was put on, and my sister Al from Australia did my makeup. I stood looking at myself in the mirror and thought, *This is it!*

My dad came and took my arm and led me downstairs where they took photos. Ross looked good in his white and blue, and my bridesmaids looked lovely in their blue dresses. Everything was going according to plan, then my dad said, "It is time to leave for church." Bob Stead was marrying Ed and I at the Manning Road Methodist Church. My sister was out from Canberra, and my aunty Joan had driven up from Uvongo. Ed's mom and sister were here from Naples; it was all about to happen.

I got into my dad's Mercedes, which was all done up with blue ribbon, and he got in, and Ross got in next to me. He drove us to the church, and it was a glorious day; the sun was shining, and I thought I could not ask for more. When we got to the church, my sister Sandy was my matron of honor and got out and pulled my train behind me and made everything look good. Ross kept saying, "Mom, you look like a princess." I took my dad's arm, and we started to walk to the door of the church. I looked inside and saw Ed in his crème suit at the front. Ross held onto his heart cushion with the rings tied on with blue ribbon.

The wedding march sounded, and we started to walk down the aisle. We got to the front, and my dad pulled my veil back and handed me over to Ed. He looked at me with all the love in his heart and took my hand. We had decided to say our own vows. So Minister Bob spoke to the congregation and then Ed said he took me to be his lawful wife to love and cherish till death us do part. Then I said my vows and promised to love and cherish him forever. After that, Bob asked Ross for the rings. We placed them on each other's fingers, and then Bob blessed us and proclaimed us husband and wife and said, "Now you may kiss the bride," which Ed did with gusto.

After that, we walked out the Church with Ross holding Ed's hand and everyone threw confetti over us as we came outside. Everyone wished us well, then we got in the car and drove to where we were having the reception, which was at the country club. We got there; and as Ed, Ross, and I came into the room, everyone was sitting down, and they all started clapping. Marco and Isabella were there, and Ed's mom kissed and hugged us and was quite taken up with Ross. Then we went for photos and came back and had our first dance. We danced to "I Will Always Love You," and Ed kissed me and then Ross came and danced with me and everyone else joined us on the dance floor. It was a lovely wedding and enjoyed by all. We cut the cake and made a wish; the cake was iced with shells as Ed and I both loved the beach. Ross fell asleep on two chairs pushed together.

We were spending the night at the Hilton Hotel, so we went to the car and Marco had put cans on the back of it and with "Just Married" written all over the car with shaving cream. We said goodbye to everyone, thanked them for coming, and got in the car. I had a blue suit on, and Ed had casual navy blue trousers and an open neck shirt on. We drove away with shouts of good luck, and the tin cans were making a noise.

When we got to the hotel, they took our car and parked it, and we were whisked off to the honeymoon suite. As we walked in, there was classical music playing and candles shining and champagne in the ice bucket. We popped the champagne, and Ed took me in his arms and said, "Tomorrow we are flying to Cape Town and staying at the Peninsula for a week." I kissed him and he kissed me back, then we drank some champagne.

I said, "Now you can wait while I go and get ready."

He said, "Don't be long."

I said, "I won't be," and I went and put on a sexy nightie. It was crème in color. I walked out of the bedroom into the room Ed was in. He came toward me and said, "You look stunning!" He kissed me and started nibbling my neck, then we made passionate love in the bedroom, and I lay in his arms afterward and said, "Well, husband, how do you feel now?" He said he is a very satisfied man and happy to have me as his wife. He said he did not want to wait to have a child so I was not on the pill. I thought we would let nature take its course. I fell asleep in Ed's arms satisfied and his wife—what more could I ask for?

We got up in the morning. Ed made us coffee, and we drank it in bed, kissing and loving each other. Then we got up and showered together and went down to breakfast. We were packed, and Marco was coming to take us in Ed's car to the airport. We had breakfast and then Marco and Isabella arrived. As they got to our table, Isabella held out her hand, and there was a diamond ring on her finger, so Marco had taken the plunge and asked her. We congratulated them then left in the car for the airport. We caught our flight with no problem, and Marco drove Ed's car back to our place as they were staying there.

We flew to Cape Town, and Ed kept holding my hand and looking at our rings. We both could hardly believe we were married now. When we landed, and they called us Mr. and Mrs. Lamparella, Ed just smiled at me; and we were whisked off in the taxi for the Peninsula Hotel. We checked in and had lunch in the dining room then walked on the beach and took some photos of table mountain, which we could see from the hotel. Ed said this was a lovely place, and I agreed with him.

We couldn't wait to get back to the room again, and soon we were peeling each other's clothes off again; it was like we couldn't get enough of each other. Soon, we were rolling around on the bed, making love. After that, we would lie naked and spent in each other's arms, drinking champagne and talking about our lives together and what we were going to do. We were going up Table Mountain tomorrow and then were booked to go to Robben Island the next day on a little boat. It was all exciting. We were both loving being together and knew it was special moments spent together as when we got back Ross would be our main concern. We intended to make the most of it while we could. Ed spoilt me horribly; he bought me a tennis bracelet with eight diamonds in it. It was lovely, and I wore it all the time.

We went up Table Mountain and loved it, and we went to Robben Island and found that very interesting. We went to the Kirstenbosch Gardens and loved that it was very pretty. For the rest of the time, we went to the beach. We loved Clifton Beach and spent the whole day there then sat watching the sunset and then walked back to the hotel and made passionate love. Ed whispered in my ear that he would love a child that would truly make him complete he did not mind if it was a boy or girl. I said, "We shall just have to wait and see if God blesses us with a precious child."

Eventually, it was Friday and the honeymoon had come to an end. We were taken to the airport and flew back to Durban. My mom and Ross were at the airport waiting and drove us home. When we got back, I made us all tea, and then we had to open all the presents. Ross loved this part. We let him open the little ones, and we all squealed with delight. I had a juicer, so was able to make us smoothies, which Ed and Ross and loved and so did I. My mom left after Ed, and I had taken her to lunch to thank her for looking after Ross, then she went home, and we went to buy some groceries. We got home, and Ed said as we sat down and had a drink he was so happy he was with the two most special people in the world to him. I said, "Good, I am glad for you. That is great." We had a lovely weekend together and then on Monday had to go back to work.

The next evening, Ed's mom and sister came for dinner, as they were leaving the next day to go back to Naples. I made Mauritian chicken curry and rice, and everyone loved it. We had a lovely evening, and his mom said she was very happy for us.

We said goodbye to them and hugged and kissed when they left as my mom was taking them to the airport as we would be at work. Ross was going with my mom; he was not going to school tomorrow. We dropped him off with my mom the next morning before we drove to work. He was happy to be going to see the airplanes. Ed and I drove to work, and I said, "What are we going to do for Christmas this year?"

And he said, "Why don't we take Ross and fly to Switzerland as that is my dream place." He said, "We could stay at a little place at the bottom of Mt. Titlis called Engelberg right in the mountains, and we could have fun in the snow. I said what a marvellous idea. He said he would Google a place for us to stay in Engelberg that day at work when he had a free moment, and when we met at lunchtime, he would have some information for me.

I went to work, and David and I worked on a big portfolio for Standard Bank all morning. When I left for lunch, I was exhausted and noticed I was getting tired very quickly. I met Ed, and we went to the Three Monkeys for lunch. We both had a toasted sandwich and a cappuccino, and Ed said he had found a lovely place for us to stay in Engelberg, which was not too expensive and included breakfast. He had also made enquiries about flights and said Ross would pay half price. I said we should go for it! Ed agreed, and we decided to leave on December 15 and come back after New Year. He said he was going back to the office and was going to book our tickets with Fawn at the travel place straight away as she said she would try and get us a discount on the airfares. I said, "Great, you do that! It will be a holiday to remember."

When I met Ed after work, he was beaming from ear to ear and said he had booked our seats on Swissair. I hugged him, and we got in the car and drove home and picked Ross up then my mom asked why should we not stay for dinner as she had put a roast in the oven, so I did not argue getting out of cooking for one night was a bonus. My dad came home and was delighted to see Ross and us there, and we had a delicious beef roast with Yorkshire pudding. All was great, and we told the folks we were going to go to Switzerland for Christmas, they were happy for us. Everything was working out. Well, his mom and sister had got off okay on their flight back to Naples and we felt like a united family now.

We hugged and kissed good night when we left, and my mom whispered in my ear that she missed us terribly. I said I missed her as well, but life was going on and we had to face forward. When we got home, we put Ross straight to bed and then Ed showed me on the computer the place he had booked for us to stay in Engelberg; it was called St. Vincent's B&B and looked stunning; the snow was all around, and they had guaranteed him it would be snowing. So we were going from the heat into the cold. We hugged each other and went to bed feeling fulfilled and happy.

Chapter 9

I went Christmas shopping at lunchtimes and organized our clothes we would need to take. We all went and bought a thick, padded jacket. Before we knew it, the day was almost here. We left work on the Friday and were flying the next day. We went home and packed then went to eat and give my folks there gifts they had invited us to eat with them as they wanted to say goodbye to us. We had drinks on the veranda as it was a hot summer evening. My mom had her Christmas tree up, and she had said Ross could open the gifts from her and my dad that night. She gave him his gift and he opened it; it was a remote red car, and he loved it. We put the batteries in it, and he played with it before we ate.

After we had said goodbye to my mom and dad and hugged and kissed them, we drove home. My folks were taking us to the airport, we were leaving at 4:00 p.m. that Saturday afternoon. We fell into bed when we got home, and I got up early and made coffee for Ed and me. We were so happy to be going on a holiday with Ross. We got up eventually after making love, and my period was late and I drove to the chemist and bought a pregnancy test. I came home and did it in the bathroom, and sure enough, it read positive. I phoned the doctor and asked for an appointment. I told Ed I was just going to get some last-minute things at the shop. I wanted to surprise him for Christmas. I went to Dr. Rodriguez, and he did a blood test and told me I was one month pregnant and the baby was due in July. He said all was fine for me to fly, and I must take care and not to ski. I could toboggan. I agreed with him and stopped at Woolworths quickly to buy something. I got home and showered and changed; we had to dress warmly. Ed had already bathed Ross, and they were both ready and dressed. We were all in denims and had our new jackets nearby to carry with us as it was too hot to put on.

My mom and dad arrived at 3:00 p.m., and we all had some tea and then packed the suitcases in the car, and off we went. Ed had wanted to buy Ross a dog, but with us going away, he said he would buy it when we came home as who would feed it, and it was a great responsibility. I agreed with him. He hugged me in the car, and Ross was so excited to be going in the big airplane. We were going to try and let him meet the pilot if we could.

When we got to the airport, we booked in and all our suitcases were underweight, which was great. Then my dad said, "Let's go and have a cup of coffee as you have forty-five minutes before you have to board or be at the gate." So we had coffee, and my mom and dad said they were going to miss us. I said we would miss them too. The next minute, it was time to board, so we walked to Gate 8 and hugged and kissed my mom and dad goodbye.

We boarded the plane and were all sitting together in the three-seater. Ross was by the window, I was in the middle, and Ed was on the aisle seat. We asked the air-hostess if Ross could meet the pilot, and she said she would see what she could do, and off she went. She came back and said we must follow her, so we did. Ross's eyes were so big and we went into the cockpit and met the pilot and the co-pilot. We saw all the lights and switches and the pilot let Ross sit on his lap for a minute and showed him how he steered the plane. It was very interesting, and then we went back to our seats and buckled up. By then, it was getting full, and then they closed the doors asked everyone to buckle up, and the next thing they showed us the emergency drill and then we were going down the runway ready to take off. I was feeling okay and had given us all a piece of chewing gum so that our ears would not pop. We took off, and soon we were in the air. Ross could see the sun and the clouds, and it was lovely to be flying above the clouds.

They brought us something to drink, and next, they were serving our dinner. We chose chicken, and Ed had beef, and it was all very tasty. After dinner had been taken away, Ed took Ross to the loo, and when they came back I went. After that, we settled Ross down as Ed had got him to do his teeth with the little toothbrush they give you on the plane. We had all brushed our teeth and then I opened Ross's blanket and put it over him, and in no time, he was asleep. I looked at Ed and was dying to tell him about the baby but had decided it was the best Christmas gift I could give him so kept it to myself and just held his hand and then touched my tummy with my other hand and thought what a miracle life is there inside our child was growing.

We arrived at Zurich airport early the next morning. They brought us breakfast, but it was too early to eat, so we just had coffee. Ed said we can get something later. We walked off the plane and put our jackets on as it was cold outside and snowing. We waited for our luggage at the luggage rail and when our suitcases came, Ed lifted them off the luggage rail onto a trolley that Ross was holding onto. We pushed the trolley to a taxi and asked them to take us to St. Vincent B&B in Engelberg. He said we would have to catch the train there, which we knew so he dropped us at the station. There was a train leaving within an hour. We went and bought tickets then saw a little coffee shop and went and had a croissant with some ham on it and some coffee. Ross had a hot chocolate. We caught the train to Engelberg, and Ross enjoyed going on the train. He was pointing out the cows and horses we saw as we went past farms; it was a lovely trip. When we got to the train station near Engelberg, we got off the train, got our suitcases, and this time, we caught a taxi to the B&B. As we arrived at St. Vincent's B&B, we were all tired. They showed us to our rooms; there were two rooms: one with one bed in it and then a double bed in another room for Ed and me.

I bathed Ross, and he was tired, and although it was only 10:00 a.m. in the morning, we needed to catch up on some sleep. I changed him into his track suit and put him in the bed. I read him a story, and Ed came and sat with him while he went off to sleep. Then Ed and I had a shower, put on our track suits, and then got into bed. We slept for a good two hours. Then we got up and got changed into our jeans, shirts, and jackets with our gloves and beanies, and we went for a little walk into the town, saw a restaurant, and decided to have lunch. We all decided to try the cheese *rostis* which were delicious. Ed had a beer and Ross and I had an appletizer.

There were all Christmas trees on with lights in the village of Engelberg, and everything was covered in snow and was white; it looked surreal. Ed and Ross had a snowball fight, and I joined in but had to be careful not to slip on the snow. We decided to eat at the B&B and go tobogganing in the morning. We went back to the B&B and sat in the bar, having a drink. Ross was allowed in there as it was quite safe, and we were only drinking appletizer. Ed was the only one drinking a beer, as were others. We then went to dinner, which was delicious. We had a hearty minestrone soup, followed by roast lamb and vegetables and potatoes or rostis, like the Swiss call them, and gravy. We then had a scrumptious bread-and-butter pudding. In two days' time, it was going to be Christmas.

We got up in the morning, and Ed made us coffee and hot chocolate for Ross, and Ross got in the bed with us; it warmed my heart to have us all together. Ross said this was a fab place! We both agreed with him, then we got up showered and got dressed and then went out with our gloves and beanies on again. We got to the snow where all the events were happening. We first went to have some breakfast, which consisted of porridge and egg and bacon and another cup of coffee. Ross said, "It sure is cold here." The hot chocolate kept him warm for a while.

We then got on a toboggan and went down a mountain; it was such fun. After that, we went into a warm place that had a fire going, and Ed ordered schnapps for him and me. I decided to have one to make Ed happy, and Ross had another hot chocolate. We then ordered a bratwurst sausage and some chips and ate it to keep us warm. We then walked along and decided to take the cable car up to Mt. Titlis. We paid for our tickets, got in the cable car, and Ross was so surprised because it really was high up. We then went up the mountain in the cable car, and Ed and Ross were squealing like girls on the way up. I took some lovely photos of all of us and then another lady took one of the three of us, and it came out well. When we got to the top, we could walk inside a glacier and that was interesting. Ross loved it, and him and Ed made snowballs again and threw them at each other. We had another hot chocolate—all of us this time, and they had marshmallows in them, which were delicious. It warmed us up, and then we caught the cable car down again. We walked back to the B&B exhausted but very happy.

That night, we were going to a special dinner as it was Christmas Eve, and we had put Ross's gift under a big Christmas tree downstairs, and at midnight, Father Christmas was going to hand the gifts out.

I could not wait to tell Ed about the baby and was lucky I had no morning sickness. We got dressed all nicely in our smart clothes and bundled up and walked down to the restaurant; they were playing Christmas music, and it was all lit up with candles and lights. The snow sure gave Christmas new meaning. We had a drink, and Ross had made friends with some other children, and they were running around. We then went into dinner, which was the ritual turkey and vegetables and mince pies and Christmas pudding.

At midnight, we were all sitting around this huge Christmas tree when Father Christmas arrived on his sleigh. He had his big bag of gifts, and they were all nicely wrapped. He started calling out names, and all the children got up as their names were called out. Eventually, it was Ross's turn, and he went up and got his gift; he ripped it open, and it was Lego, his favorite. He was so excited that he came and hugged Ed and me. Ed said my gift was this holiday, and I said, "Guess what?" He looked at me and shook his head. I went up to him and whispered in his ear that I was pregnant. He looked at me then took me in his arms and kissed me so fast it took my breath away.

He was so delighted; he said, "Let's tell Ross." So we went back to our table; he called Ross over, and he sat on Ed's knee and then he told him I was having a baby. Ross was so happy; he was glad that he was going to have a brother or sister. Then Ed said no more tobogganing for me and looked at me and said, "Now my life is complete."

A new life, and both Ross and I in his life, what more could he ask for? I said, "Yes, the new life of this baby was the best Christmas gift one could get and the greatest gift of all."

www.ingramcontent.com/pod-product-compliance
Lightning Source LLC
Chambersburg PA
CBHW051234210726
48290CB00003B/962